# GUARDIANS
## of GA'HOOLE

# The Hatchling

D1016189

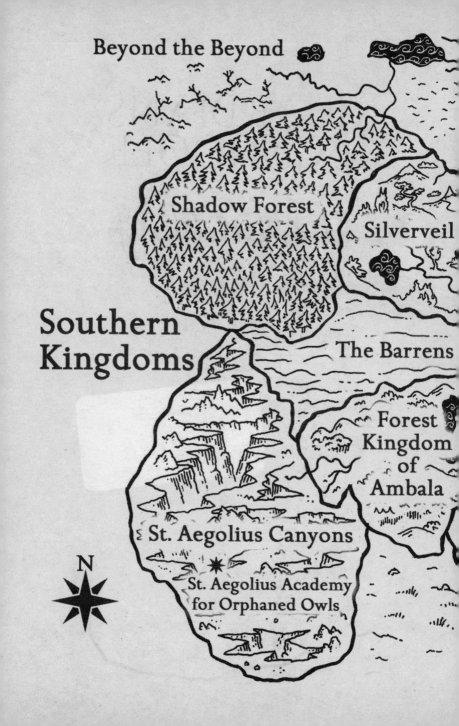

*The young'un was seeing something. The old Rogue smith could tell by the way Nyroc's eyes stared, unblinking, into the gizzard of this fire. Gwyndor studied the reflection of the flames in Nyroc's eyes. He felt his own gizzard give a twang. Was it the Ember of Hoole he saw reflected in those young eyes?*

# GUARDIANS
## *of* GA'HOOLE

BOOK SEVEN

## *The Hatchling*

BY KATHRYN LASKY

SCHOLASTIC INC.

New York  Toronto  London  Auckland  Sydney
Mexico City  New Delhi  Hong Kong  Buenos Aires

*For Maria Weisbin*

ISBN 0-439-73950-0

Text copyright © 2005 by Kathryn Lasky. All rights reserved. Published by Scholastic Inc. SCHOLASTIC and associated logos are trademarks and/or registered trademarks of Scholastic Inc.

Artwork by Richard Cowdrey
Design by Steve Scott

12 11 10 9 8 7 6 5 4 3 2          5 6 7 8 9 10/0

Printed in the U.S.A.      40

First printing, June 2005

# Northern Kingdoms

N

Glauxian Brothers
Retreat

Bitter
Sea

Kiel Bay

Stormfast Island

Bay of Fangs

Everwinter Sea

Ice Talons

Ice
Narrows

Dark Fowl Island

Southern
Kingdoms

# Contents

# Prologue

"It's the hatchling," a young owl said as the group watched Nyroc, only son of the great warrior Kludd, begin a power dive. He grasped a charred branch from the ground in his beak and in one swift movement rose seamlessly again into the air brandishing it before him. He had performed the retrieval perfectly and was swinging the branch with great style. And this was just his first flight. A power dive on a first flight was an outrageous and daring maneuver to attempt and he had executed it flawlessly. He then carved a perfect figure eight in the sky above the two large peaks known as the Great Horns. This was followed by spiraling descent to a slide-in landing on the ledge where his elders perched. His angle of approach was superb. Then, in front of his mother and her top lieutenants, the hatchling raised his starboard wing and shreed, "Hail, Kludd! Supreme Commander of the Tytonic Union of Pure Ones! Hail, Her Pureness General Mam, Nyra, beloved mate of the late High Tyto Kludd!"

# CHAPTER ONE

# A Perfect Son

M agnificent!" exclaimed an older owl.
"And to think that he has been flying for only a few nights."

"I've never seen the 'Hail, Kludd' so perfectly executed," whispered another Barn Owl.

"General Mam, you should be proud of your son. Nyroc is the perfect young Pure One. He shall soon be able to serve in the most elite of the Tytonic Union's forces."

"Yes," Nyra replied softly. She almost breathed the word. Her hatchling had exceeded her wildest expectations. She had lost much in the cataclysmic battle against the evil owl troops known as the Guardians of Ga'Hoole. Her mate, Kludd, the High Tyto of the Pure Ones, had been killed. But she had been blessed two nights later when Nyroc, her and Kludd's chick, had hatched. Not only was the hatchling the first to be born to the High Tyto, he had hatched on a rare night when the shadow of the earth came between the moon and the sun, the night of an eclipse. His mother, too, had been hatched on such a night. Because of this, he had been given a special name, Nyroc, the one given to all male hatchlings born under the shadowed moon. Nyra told him that owls hatched on these nights were destined to have great powers.

Nyroc remembered that moment perfectly. His mum had brought her huge white face, unusually large for a Barn Owl, close to his. It appeared as large as a moon itself. Pure glistening white with a seam that ran diagonally across it, a scar from a long-ago battle wound. This was Nyroc's first memory: the moon in the sky being eaten by the shadow of the earth, and the moon of his mother's face hovering over him. In his confusion Nyroc had thought that the moon had dropped from the sky and was speaking to him. He recalled those first words his mum spoke even though he only half understood them. "I shall call you the name of all male chicks hatched at the time of the eclipse," she said. "I name you Nyroc, my hatchling." Then she nodded toward a set of burnished metal claws that hung against the stone wall of their hollow. "You shall grow into those claws, Nyroc, your father's battle claws. They are the sacred relics of the Pure Ones. You were born to wear them into battle. Regard them closely, my hatchling."

Every night, as his mum told him of the magnificent

feats of his father in battle, Nyroc fastened his gaze on the great battle claws. They seemed to glow with an intensity that matched a full-shine moon. And each night, Nyra would conclude her battle claw stories with these words: "You shall bring to these claws great honor. You shall grow up to be strong and fierce like your father."

But the little hatchling was becoming much more. Some said he might prove even greater than Kludd. There was now only a remnant left of the original Tytonic Union of Pure Ones. Their defeat in the battle known as The Burning had been decisive, humiliating, and complete. Or so the rest of owlkind thought.

But this young hatchling, the one called Nyroc, was the hope — the greatest hope of the Pure Ones. The tarnished destiny of their Union would be polished bright with the hatchling's power, his skill, and his agility. The other young owls who had recently been lured to the Union wilfed as they witnessed Nyroc's unbelievable performance. How would they ever live up to this paragon of Tytonic splendor? They almost resented him, but that was a very dangerous sentiment to allow oneself to feel. Instead, they clacked their beaks loudly along with the other owls in a loud ovation of admiration that bordered on the ecstatic. Nyroc was indeed "perfect."

"He has the moves, by Glaux! He has the moves. Great

Glaux in glaumora, that power dive for the branch! I have no doubt had it been ignited he would have astonished us further." It was the tough old lieutenant commander Uglamore who spoke now. And Uglamore should know. He and Stryker were among the few left from the elite forces who had faced the flame squadrons of Ga'Hoole and survived.

Fighting with fire was not a natural thing for the Pure Ones. They had had to force themselves to learn. The Ga'Hoolian owls, however, were experts. Manipulation of fire was a crucial part of their culture. They not only forged weapons and tools and used it to light the Great Tree, they had a team, the colliering chaw, that dove into forest fires to retrieve coals. And nobody was better at this than the Ga'Hoolian owl called Soren — the brother — and murderer — of Kludd.

Of course all such talk of the Great Tree was strictly forbidden. Under the threat of the most severe punishment, no owl of the Union was ever to speak of the Great Tree, or the legends of the Great Tree. Knowledge of the tree was considered "spronk," the owl word for forbidden.

It was with added excitement that Nyra viewed the aerial displays of her son, for they proved he would indeed be their redeemer and the one to wreak vengeance on Soren. He had been told as much since birth. And his gizzard quickened to the task. At twixt time, when the last gray tatters of the darkness dissolve into the pale pinks of the dawn, when owls finish their night's work and get ready for sleep, his mum had told him stories of how his da, Kludd, had died at the fiery talons of his uncle Soren. It was their twixt time ritual, a kind of prayer they chanted together now, for Nyroc knew the words so well.

The lives of owls were filled with ceremonies that marked important events from an owl's hatching to its death and the Final ceremony. Nyroc had already performed many of these rites. He had gone through the First Meat ceremony, when an owlet eats something other than a worm or a bug for the first time. This had been quickly followed by the First Fur ceremony, when Nyroc first ate his fresh-killed meat with the fur still on it. Next was the First Bones ceremony, when the young hatchling had been deemed mature enough to eat his meat with the bones. Then came the all-important First Pellet ceremony. The fur and bones were packed into a tight little bundle in the gizzard of the owl and then it was "yarped" or expelled through the beak. Because of this neat way of ridding themselves of most of their waste materials, owls considered themselves to have the noblest digestive systems in the bird kingdom. They commonly referred to all other birds as wet poopers.

Today's First Flight was one of the most important of all the ceremonies and because Nyroc had passed it with such astounding success, he would be permitted to go on to the next ceremony, First Prey, then finally the one that was mysteriously called the Special, or sometimes "Tupsi."

Cries of "Perfect! Perfection!" rang out. "This is the most perfect example of what our young P.O. Youths should be." The other young owls wilfed again as they heard their elders exclaiming over Nyroc's performance.

But there was one, a small Sooty Owl, who did not wilf. Indeed, he seemed to experience quite the opposite reaction. He puffed up and appeared especially pleased with the hatchling's performance. This owl was known as Dustytuft. In the rigid ordering that defined the Pure Ones' society he occupied one of the lowest ranks.

Any owl who joined this odd Union of Barn Owls, who claimed to be the purest owls in the entire owl universe, soon learned that some Barn Owls were considered more pure than others. Of the many kinds of Barn Owls, the purest were thought to be the Tyto alba, the Barn Owls with the heart-shaped white faces like Nyroc, his mother, and Uglamore and Stryker. Beneath them in the social order of the Pure Ones were the Masked Owls whose heart-shaped faces were not pure white. Then came the Grass Owls, with even darker heart-shaped faces. Toward the bottom of the rankings were the Greater Sooties, like Dustytuft, and lowest of all, beneath the Greater Sooties, were the Lesser Sooties.

Dustytuft, like all Greater Sooties, known more formally as Tyto tenebricosa, looked as if he'd been sprinkled with coal dust, leaving only a few white spots flecking his darker upper parts. His face was not precisely heart-shaped but looked a little more squashed.

It was Dustytuft's particular misfortune in life to have been born into this second-lowest order of Tytos. Indeed, until the hatching of Nyroc, Dustytuft thought himself to be the most miserable owl in the world. He had never wanted to join the Union. It had been his father's idea. After the great forest fire in Silverveil in which the rest of his family had perished, his father had gone a bit yoicks and felt their future lay with the powerful and mysterious group of owls known as the Pure Ones. His father had then gotten himself killed in his first battle, a minor skirmish with a small group of Ga'Hoolian owls.

It was not long after his father's death that Dustytuft began to understand how truly awful it was to be a Sooty Owl within the Union of the Purest. His formal name might include the word Tyto, but it seemed to count for nothing. With no father and a lineage considered less pure, less noble than those Tytos who ranked above him, he had been given all of the worst jobs. They would not even allow him to be called by his real name, which he had forgotten although he was certain it had been something quite distinguished. The Pure Ones had renamed him Dustytuft. All Sooties had similar dirty-sounding names, such as Muddy Wings or Ash Beak. Even now there was a Lesser Sooty named Smutty being held prisoner for supposed cowardice in the face of the enemy. Theirs was not an enviable lot. And if Dusty had said "it ain't fair" once, he had said it a thousand times.

But all that had changed when the hatchling was born. It had seemed just short of miraculous at the time, how Dustytuft had been summoned to attend the hatching. And then ever since that momentous occasion when the earth slid between the moon and the sun, it was as if Dustytuft himself had slipped into a new, more exalted orbit within the solar system that was known as the Tytonic Union of Pure Ones. His fortunes had definitely changed. He was asked to attend to the young hatchling at every important ceremony. Indeed, he and Nyroc had become the best of friends.

So while other young owls wilfed at Nyroc's flawless performances in every task required to prove himself a fearless and worthy member of the Tytonic Union, Dustytuft rejoiced in his companion's accomplishments.

He himself would never be tested in this way. He would never be permitted to even dream of being a member of the most elite forces like the scouts or the Fire Talons. He would never be measured for a pair of battle claws to be made by a Rogue smith. But now it didn't matter. He was the companion and best friend to Nyroc, future leader of the Pure Ones, heir to the most feared title in the owl kingdom — High Tyto!

# CHAPTER TWO

# A Reprimand

Y ou what?" Nyra screeched.

*Uh-oh!* thought Nyroc.

"You dare question me about why that Lesser Sooty is a prisoner?"

"I'm sorry, General Mam. I . . . I . . . thought . . ."

"You *didn't* think. When I say someone is a coward, he is a coward. And that is exactly what Smutty is — a coward. Not only that, he violated the code of spronk."

"You mean he said something about the Great Ga'Hoole Tree?"

Nyra flinched as Nyroc said the words. "Yes," she hissed.

"That's awful, Mum."

Ever since Nyroc remembered, talk of the Great Tree, except in the most scathing and derogatory terms, was absolutely forbidden. His mother had drummed this lesson into him so completely that whenever the word "Ga'Hoole" was mentioned Nyroc's ear slits automatically sealed.

This blistering reprimand occurred minutes after Nyroc completed his flawless First Flight ceremony when mother and son were alone in the stone hollow they shared in the cleft of a high cliff. It had been stupid of him to question her. He was never supposed to question his mum.

Although he was barely two months old, Nyroc the hatchling knew that his mother's moods were unpredictable. One minute he could be basking in the warm glow of her pride and the next minute he was scorched by her anger. Dustytuft had tried to explain it to him many times. "It's because she loves you so much, Nyroc. And there are things about you that remind her so much of your dear dead da. It must be hard for her. She has great expectations and you know, well . . . sometimes she just gets a little intense."

"What's intense?" Nyroc asked. Dustytuft was older than Nyroc and knew a lot more.

"Well, it just means she gets kind of desperate. She's proud of you. She really is."

Dustytuft always made Nyroc feel better. Nyroc didn't know what he would do without him. For one thing, his life would be very lonely, for none of the other young owls who had been recruited into the Pure Ones seemed to like Nyroc. He sensed their resentment. For the most part he didn't care. He just wanted to be the best Pure One he could be. He wanted to be exactly like his da. Even though his da had been killed before he was born, after all the wonderful stories his mother had told him of his father's greatness, he felt as if he knew him. His only real desire in life was to be as great a leader as Kludd. He felt it was his destiny, although he was not quite sure exactly what that strange word — destiny — meant.

Nyroc was not only an expert flier for such a young owl but he was an expert at something else — erasing unpleasant thoughts from his mind. It was probably this more than anything else that made him a model young owl in the small but growing cadre of young owls being trained to restore the glory of the Union. So that is exactly what he did now: He erased Nyra's anger by basking in the glow of his recent achievement.

His mother was a stern and unforgiving flight instructor. But how he loved her for that now. He churred softly to himself when he thought of those first lessons. Since the Battle of The Burning the primary element that owls used in their First Flight exercises was missing — trees. Young chicks, unless they had been hatched in the desert, usually began their flying lessons by "branching" or hopping from branch to branch. But since that last battle, the trees of the canyonlands — which had been sparse to begin with — were reduced to charred, jagged stumps. So there was no hopping from limb to limb for Nyroc but from rock to rock or ledge to ledge. It had not been a problem for him. Within a day he was managing short flights between rock ledges. But his mum was always demanding that he fly faster, and criticized his turns, which she said were messy, not worthy of a "drunk pigeon."

He gave another churr, the owl form of laughter, when he recalled this. He hadn't minded flying faster but it made so much noise when he did it. The soft fringe feathers, unique to most owls, were responsible for the lovely silent flight at slower speeds, which he so enjoyed. But his mother insisted that he fly silently at ever greater speeds. Nyra herself was a very noisy flier although she thought she was quite silent. Nyroc could hear her coming in from a league away. She flapped in as noisily as a duck. But not Nyroc. He finally mastered the art of flying fast and silently. That was another bit of praise he had heard from the elders at the ceremony. "So fast! So quiet! Unbelievably gifted!" And another exclaimed, "Swift as an eagle. Silent as an owl. Truly brilliant. Just what we need to rebuild the empire."

Nyra, too, had heard this last remark and it pleased her. Not counting the new untrained recruits, there were barely twenty Pure Ones left since the last battle, but it was from these remnants that Nyra hoped to rebuild that empire of greatness, the Tytonic Union, that she and Kludd had ruled. Their past victories had been magnificent. They had invaded and ruled St. Aggie's, the small but powerful stronghold to the south of where they now were, that possessed an important natural resource — flecks — which could be used to control the minds and gizzards of other owls. But at the last battle with the Guardians of Ga'Hoole, St. Aggie's had been lost and those flecks had somehow been rendered powerless by the raging fires.

Nyra had flown out on an errand after reprimanding Nyroc and was now back at the hollow in the cleft. She had completely forgotten about her son's insolent question. She was telling him how all the elders were raving about his performance. "They cannot believe your elegance and speed, my dear. You are perfection, but even perfection can be improved. Those new recruits who have been flying longer than you wish they were nearly as good."

"Really, Mum?"

"Oh, yes, really. You should be so proud."

Nyroc thought about this for a moment. Then he nodded. "If I am like you and if I am like my da, yes, then I am proud." It was the perfect answer. Nyra beamed.

Nyroc often wondered if other owlets' mothers were like his. Maybe not. But then again other owlets were not destined to become great leaders as he was.

"You see," his mum continued, "it is very important that you do everything just as I say, because soon your Special ceremony will be coming up. Your Tupsi."

Nyroc was not exactly sure what Tupsi was. He thought it might be connected to something with the prisoner, Smutty, but he certainly didn't want to bring that Lesser Sooty up again, for that was what had caused his mum's violent outburst. "What exactly is the Special ceremony, Mum? And why do they call it Tupsi?"

"When I think you are ready, I'll tell you all about it and after that ceremony you shall become an officer in the army of the Pure Ones. Oh, your father would have been so proud." She sighed. "But before that we shall have the Marking, the Final ceremony for your father."

"When will that be, Mum?"

"As soon as Uglamore and Wortmore can find a Rogue smith."

"You mean, for fire?" Nyroc said excitedly.

"Yes, my dear. Your father's bones are all that is left now, and they must be burned because the Final ceremonies of great leaders require fire. It is called the Marking."

Nyroc felt a tremor of excitement in his gizzard. The Pure Ones did not know how to make fire themselves. They relied entirely on lightning strikes and Rogue smiths. Rogue smiths not only knew how to make fires that could be controlled but they made hotter fires in which weapons such as battle claws could be made. Although this land in which Nyroc had hatched had been scorched and made treeless and ugly by fire, he was fascinated with the notion that an owl could make fire — small fires with which useful things could be fashioned. He knew that the evil owls of Ga'Hoole were able to make their own weapons and much more with their fires. Nyroc had never even seen a real fire. He had seen only the blackened landscape it had left behind.

Almost as much as he wished to see fire, Nyroc wanted to see a tree, a real tree that was growing and not a charred stump. He had heard rumors of trees with leaves and hollows in which owls could live, hollows that were lined with soft moss. There was no moss in these canyonlands since The Burning. Dustytuft had often tried to describe moss to him, its softness and its colors, which were all shades of green. There was one so soft it was called rabbit's ear moss. But Nyroc did not even know what the color green was. There was much to ponder in this life — the color green, fire, the rumor of trees in distant places, the softness of moss, and the meaning of the word "destiny."

# CHAPTER THREE
## The Marking

Twenty owls swooped down into the narrow canyon. Nyra was in the lead with Nyroc and Uglamore just behind her. Dustytuft flew next to Nyroc. Once again, Dustytuft was amazed at his exalted position in this group of top lieutenants from the old elite forces for this solemn ceremony — the Marking, the Final ceremony for fallen leaders. That is, Dustytuft thought, fallen leaders whose bodies could be recovered. Too often the vultures got to the dead soldiers first, or if an owl was fatally wounded over the Hoolemere Sea, the body was never found.

But Kludd had been killed in a cave battle. His body, of which only the bones now remained, had been guarded night and day until a Rogue smith could be found to perform the Marking. Nyroc had never before been to the cave. He was apprehensive. He was to see for the first time the bones of his father; his father, in whose powerful wing thrusts he was to follow; his father, the greatest leader the

Tytonic Union had ever known; his father, whose fierceness in battle caused every owl's gizzard to quiver. His father, killed by his own dreadful brother, Soren, in a battle of fire and ice with the Guardians of Ga'Hoole. Yes, Nyroc was very nervous and perhaps for this reason his mother had allowed Dustytuft to fly so close to him. Even now as they entered the huge cave and the shadows seemed to reach out for them, Nyra made sure that there was a space for Dustytuft near Nyroc.

*Things sure have changed,* Dustytuft thought. *I used to be just some no-account owl.* But now he was favored!

They flew toward the rear of the cave and took their places on a ledge. Some white sticks had been arranged on the cave floor. And propped against a rock was the metal mask that his father had always worn to cover his war-mutilated face. His mum had said that his father's other name was Metal Beak. It was one of the first goodlight stories she had told him when he was a very young hatchling. She liked to tell stories of his father's great bravery and feats in battle. But he found this one frightening. He didn't like thinking that his father had a face he would have never seen. "But, Mum," he once asked, "would he have had to talk to me through that metal beak?"

"Of course. It gave his voice a lovely resonance." Nyroc didn't know what resonance was and he didn't ask.

His mum patted him along now with her outstretched wing. "Follow me, Nyroc," she said. "We must nod pule to your father."

"Nod pule, what's that?" Nyroc asked.

"Pay your respects, give homage."

"You mean, say good-bye?" Nyroc asked.

"Yes!" his mum snapped. "Now stop asking so many questions."

*Oh, goodness,* Nyroc thought, *this is not the time to frink her off. I better shut up.* But he couldn't help but ask one more question. "Can Dustytuft come, too?"

"Of course, darling. Dustytuft can always come." Dustytuft blinked at this. *Downright miracle,* he thought. The Sooty Owl puffed up his chest a bit.

"Thanks, Mum."

Nyroc's next question — if he had dared to ask — would have been "What do we say good-bye to?"

He soon found out. The white things on the cave floor that he thought were sticks were actually his father's bones. A large shaggy Masked Owl stood by them. Near the Masked Owl's talons was a small metal bucket. Nyroc knew from Dustytuft that this was the bucket in which all Rogue smiths carried their live coals or embers. Nyroc stole a glance into it and saw the bright orange glow. A shiver ran through his gizzard like nothing he had ever felt before. But suddenly, there was a sharp peck on his back and Nyra hissed, "Pay attention! These are your father's bones." And then she added, "Do you see the one in the middle?"

"Yes," Nyroc replied.

"You see how it is broken in two?"

"Yes," he said again.

"That was his spine. Soren, your father's brother — your uncle — dealt the deathblow that split his spine. I want you to remember that. Never, ever forget."

"Yes, Mum."

"Promise!" she said fiercely.

"I promise, Mum. I promise. I'll never forget."

Dustytuft knew what bones were. Dustytuft knew about dying and death and owls killed in battle. But what preoccupied Dustytuft right now was why he was a guest at this sacred ceremony. It was an honor far beyond the strange favoritism Nyra had granted him since Nyroc's hatching. After all, Nyra had been furious with him and all the Sooty Owls after the Pure Ones had lost the Battle of The Burning to the Guardians of Ga'Hoole. There was a Lesser Sooty in prison right now for supposed coward-ice. One might have thought that these Sooty Owls were the reason the Pure Ones had lost. In truth, the Sooties were such lowly owls they had hardly been given any responsibilities. It was as if she was so angered by the defeat that she simply had to blame someone. Nyra's anger could be immense.

But two days after the battle, when Nyroc had hatched, Nyra had invited Dustytuft into the nest in the cleft of the rock to chick-sit while she went off hunting. This was a great honor. Dustytuft had liked Nyroc right from the start. Their friendship began to grow, and Nyra encouraged it. Dustytuft felt so close to Nyroc that he confessed to him one of his innermost secrets, which was that he hated the name the Pure Ones had chosen for him. Once, he told Nyroc, he had had a real name. He thought it had been something rather noble-sounding, like Edgar or Phillip. And Nyroc had asked him which name he liked the best. No one had ever asked him such a personal question. He thought for a minute and said, "Phillip — definitely Phillip." So when no one was about, Nyroc called Dustytuft Phillip. It was the one thing that Nyroc did that was less than perfect, in the Pure-One sense of the word. It was odd that this one flaw in Nyroc's otherwise perfect behavior was what Dustytuft most admired him for, and what, unlike Nyra's strange favoritism, made Dustytuft feel truly honored. He had said to Nyroc many times that it was too much of a risk. But Nyroc had simply shrugged it off and told him not to worry. "I'll call you Phillip and make up for it by being extra good in everything else." And he had.

Now the Sooty Owl stood beside Nyroc and looked down at the bones of the owl that had been Kludd, High Tyto of the Pure Ones. He could see that Nyroc was, even after his mum's reprimand, still stealing looks at the Rogue smith and his bucketful of embers, which seemed to interest the hatchling more than his father's bones. Perhaps, mused Dustytuft, Nyroc was even less perfect than he knew. He had never seen Nyroc disobey his mother like this. Luckily, she wasn't watching. Her attention was riveted on the bones.

"And now the time has come to honor our fallen leader in the manner befitting a great soldier," Uglamore intoned. Nyra motioned Nyroc to step back toward the wall of the cave. Uglamore kept talking, as Gwyndor, the Rogue smith, came up to the place where the bones of Kludd lay and spread some dry twigs and bark over them. He took an ember from his bucket and set it on the twigs. Flames sprang up from the bones. The darkness of the cave began to flash and sparkle. Suddenly, shadows began leaping and sliding through the cave. Nyroc blinked. Never had he seen such shadows. They were huge. The flickering light of the fire made them jigger and jump in an odd dance across the stone walls of the cave. A bright realization flooded Nyroc's mind. *It is light that makes shadows. Look to the light. Look to the flames.* Then he looked into the flames. His gizzard lurched. *I am supposed to be seeing the bones of my father burning,* he thought. *But I am seeing something else.*

Nyroc saw a landscape he did not recognize. And across this land, creatures with four legs and peculiarly colored eyes loped. The fire was crackling loudly now but beneath its hisses and snapping Nyroc thought he heard low growls. Darker shapes like gray mist floated through the air above the four-legged creatures. Then he saw something else. His gizzard gave a deep strange quiver, and he felt a pull deep within himself. He peered harder into the fire. It seemed at first like one of the fire's flames. It was orange and at its center there was a lick of deep blue like the sky on a clear day. As he looked closer, Nyroc saw yet another color around the edge of the blue. It was the same color as the creatures' eyes. Was this green? Was this a leaf? Was this the color Dustytuft had tried to describe when he spoke of trees? Something about the tricolor shape still hovering in the dancing flames entranced Nyroc and he could not look away. He felt himself being pulled to this flame. He imagined himself plunging into it, diving right into its center.

Nyra was chanting a song for fallen warriors and the

other owls were watching her, all except for Gwyndor, the Rogue smith. He was watching Nyroc.

The young'un was seeing something. The old Rogue smith could tell by the way Nyroc's eyes stared, unblinking, into the gizzard of this fire. Gwyndor studied the reflection of the flames in Nyroc's eyes. He felt his own gizzard give a twang. Was it the Ember of Hoole he saw reflected in those young eyes? Gwyndor, like all blacksmiths, looked upon fires as living creatures with an anatomy not entirely different from that of an owl. Just as owls had gizzards in which they felt their deepest emotions, fires had gizzards, too. There were some owls who had the gift to look right into the flames of a fire and find that gizzard, and with this came a special kind of vision. Few had it. Gwyndor did not. Even Bubo, the blacksmith of the Great Ga'Hoole Tree, did not possess it. Orf, who crafted the finest battle claws in the world on the remote island of Dark Fowl, was said to have it. Long ago, there had been a very few colliers who were said to be able to see a fire's gizzard. Still, none of these had ever been able to find the legendary Ember of Hoole. There had been many stories about the Ember and the powers it held within its deepest blue. It was a blue like the color of the bonk embers that the smiths favored for their hottest fires. But the Ember of Hoole was more than just a bonk ember. Much more.

Gwyndor had never seen an owl stare so deeply into the flames. And such a young owl at that! What was he seeing in that fire? The Rogue smith had not wanted to come to the canyonlands. He had no desire to have any dealings with the Pure Ones. Since the last battle, The Burning, he had wanted to fly clear of this very odd group of owls who had such strange beliefs about the pureness of Barn Owls. He had been quite surprised that the little Sooty was permitted to stand so close to the son of the great fallen leader, Kludd. There wasn't a Rogue smith around when Kludd lived who had not been called upon to fashion a mask or claws for him or his followers.

Gwyndor now wondered why he had come here—all the way from Ambala. He remembered the night that he decided to go. Earlier in the evening he had visited the strange little Spotted Owl called Mist where she lived with the eagles. It had been rumored for years that Mist was actually the legendary Hortense, hero of Ambala, because of the undaunted courage she had shown when she had worked as a slipgizzle, years ago at St. Aggie's. The heroism of Hortense was so much a part of the lore and history of Ambala that almost every other owl you met there, male or female, had been named after her. Gwyndor was not sure if Mist was or was not the real Hortense. All he knew was that he enjoyed her company when he went to visit the eagles. She was so elderly now and so faded that she did in fact seem more mist than owl. Gwyndor had noticed that after visiting with her he would often have strange dreams, dreams that he could never entirely remember.

And that had been the case on the night after his last visit to Mist. Uglamore and Wortmore, two lieutenants of the Pure Ones, had already asked him, and a half dozen other Rogue smiths, if they would come to do the Marking for the Final ceremony for Kludd. He had at first refused, as had the others. But on the night after that visit with Mist, he had woken up at tween time after having had another strange dream and decided — for no apparent reason — that he should go to the canyonlands and do this small service for the Pure Ones, even if he did not like Nyra or the rest of the group. In some way that dream he could no longer remember had instilled deep in his gizzard an urge to go.

Now he wondered if this little owlet, the one they called the hatchling, who was staring so intently into the fire, was the reason he had been summoned here. Yes, summoned. That was the word. He had felt there was something beyond the Marking duties that he would need to do here. *This isn't about dead bones at all,* he suddenly realized. He regarded Nyroc, whose unusually large white face, so similar to his mother's, hung like a moon in the glimmering orange shadows of the cave. *This is about him. But what am I supposed to do?*

"*Time will tell,*" a voice seemed to whisper as if from a dimly remembered dream. "*Time will tell.*"

# CHAPTER FOUR

## First Prey

Nyroc could not get the flames out of his mind. He had never seen anything quite like it. It seemed to him that the flames in some way told a story, or at least part of a story. Where was this land? What were those loping creatures? And was that color around the core of that tricolor flame really green? There was something else that he had glimpsed in the fire but not clearly. It was frightening. He almost did not want to see it. He felt it had something to do with his terrible uncle Soren. But he could not be sure.

"Nyroc!" his mum screeched. "Pay attention. I'm letting you navigate while we track this chipmunk, and you're not listening at all. What's happened to you lately? Very inattentive! Won't do, Nyroc. Won't do at all. If you can't even follow a chipmunk, how are you ever going to track a mouse, which is much smaller? You must start using those lovely Glaux-given ear slits."

To demonstrate, Nyra tipped her head one way then another.

"You're right, General Mam, as always. I have been distracted." Nyroc was replying mechanically in just the tone his mum expected after a reprimand. It signaled total obedience. "I offer no excuses except that I was deeply moved by my great father's Marking ceremony."

He blinked three times. His mother's words came back to him. *You shall grow into your father's battle claws, Nyroc. They are the sacred relic of the Pure Ones. You are the only one fit to wear them into battle. Regard them closely, my hatchling.*

Nyroc was indeed inspired. He could imagine the claws sinking into flesh in battle. And this, now, was his first battle — his First Prey ceremony. He began to swing his head just as his mother had demonstrated in the lesson on directional ear slit maneuvering. Within seconds he had picked up the noise of scampering feet. It was coming from his downwind side. His left ear was receiving the sound before his right ear. He angled his tail and began to fly in the direction of the noise source. It was the chipmunk, he was fairly sure. The sound of the chipmunk's feet and then its breathing came to both ear slits at almost the same time. There was only the difference of a fraction of a second.

In another three seconds, Nyroc had begun the plunging kill-spiral. While spiraling, he managed to stay with the prey — silently. The ground rushed toward him, but Nyroc kept his eyes on the striped back of the little chipmunk.

The squeak as Nyroc sank his talons into the fleshy sides of the rodent was very tiny—more a squeak of surprise than pain. Even so, for a creature that small there was an awful lot of blood. Overhead he heard cheers. He had not known that others would be attending his First Prey ceremony. But Uglamore, Wortmore, and Dustytuft, of course, and the Rogue smith Gwyndor were flying above in a circle formation to welcome the new hunter.

"Hooray! Hooray! You got your first prey!" The cheer rang out into the darkening night. Nyra took the dying animal from his talons and squeezed the blood from it over Nyroc's head. When they returned to their rocky nest, Nyroc's white face was red with the chipmunk's blood. His gizzard squirmed uncomfortably as he felt the mask of blood drying, tightening on his face.

There was a celebration that night on the ledges between the Great Horns, the two peaks that rose like the tufts of a Great Horned Owl into the starry sky. Nyroc saw his mum in deep conversation with Gwyndor. She saw her son perched off to one side, alone and in deep thought. She came up to him and gave him a gentle swat. The other owls his age were off in playful flights riding the thermals off the Great Horns. They had not invited Nyroc to join them. "Don't be a spoilsport, dear. This is your celebration. You don't look happy at all. What in Glaux are you thinking about?"

Nyroc hesitated a minute while he commanded another thought to enter his head so he would not have to tell his mother what he was truly thinking about. He knew this was close to lying. He had never told a lie before, never even dreamed of it, and especially not to his mum. "You really want to know, Mum?"

"Of course I want to know."

"Green," Nyroc said quietly. "I was thinking about green."

Nyra blinked and then narrowed her eyes. Sometimes her son confounded her. She would perceive a glimmer of something in him that made her uneasy. He was so disciplined. She credited herself for developing that in him, but how could such a controlled mind be thinking about something so ridiculous as green? "Green? Green what?" she screeched.

"Green, the color green. I want to know what green is."

"Leaves are green," Nyra said with exasperation.

"But I've never seen a leaf. Everything is burnt up around here."

"Well, someday, after your Special ceremony — if you

perform your Special ceremony in a brave manner—I'll fly you to a place so you can see a living tree."

"Really, Mum? Really! Oh, Mum, I love you sooo much."

Nyra looked at him strangely. Where did he learn these things? These words like "love"?

Later during the celebration when he and Dustytuft were riding the thermals, Nyroc spotted his mum on a ledge below in deep conversation with Gwyndor again.

"Dustytuft, what's Mum talking to Gwyndor about, and how come he's still here? I thought he had just come for the Marking at the Final ceremony."

"I'm not sure. Rumor has it that she is trying to get him to make some fire claws."

"What are fire claws?" Nyroc asked.

"The deadliest kind of battle claws. Somehow they put a live coal in the tip of each claw. It allows a soldier to fight within intense heat at very close range."

"Glaux. It sounds exciting! Have you ever fought with them?"

Dusty blinked. "Of course not. You don't think they would give a lowly Sooty Owl such a powerful weapon?"

"Oh, Phillip," Nyroc said softly. "I'm going to talk to Mum about getting you promoted."

"That's very kind of you, Nyroc, but I don't think it'll work."

"Why not? She's let you become my best friend."

"Yes," Dustytuft replied, trying not to let his voice quaver or betray his anxiety. This special treatment by Nyra was still confounding him. That she would let her precious hatchling become such good friends with a Sooty Owl was not easily explained.

# CHAPTER FIVE

# What Does This Youngun See?

It was a chilly dawn and normally Nyroc's mum would have been there all fluffy and cozy to nestle up against. She had been there a short time before when they had nestled in for their day sleep. It was most unusual for his mum to be gone at this hour. Nyroc stood up a little straighter. He cocked his head one way and then the other. He heard whisperings from a ledge several feet below him. In the pit of a stone well there were the twigs and curls of bark laid out.

"Look here, Gwyndor," Nyra was saying. "Isn't this a perfect place for a forge? I had my lieutenants bring in this kindling for you. I think you could get a fire going hot enough for some good fire claws."

"It's not that, madam."

"Well then, what is it?"

"It's difficult to explain. But I am not comfortable making the claws."

"Battle claws, be they fire claws or not, have never been a matter of comfort."

"But they do bad things to the Glaux-given talons we have. They scorch and ruin your talons, madam."

"But they kill so well!" Nyra replied harshly, and then blinked at Gwyndor as if he were the stupidest creature in the world.

"Yes. That they do."

"Hi, Mum," Nyroc said as he lighted down next to the spot where Nyra and Gwyndor were talking.

"What are you doing here? You have no business being out of the hollow at this time of the morning," his mum said sharply.

Gwyndor backed away and pretended to be fiddling with something in his blacksmith's kit.

"I just wanted to ask you one question, Mum."

"What is it now?" Nyra gave him a withering look. *Questions again! Always questions. Too many questions*, she thought. That is what confounded her, made her uneasy about her son.

"I was wondering if . . . maybe you would consider promoting Dustytuft? You know, not to a lieutenant or anything but maybe a sublieutenant."

Nyra looked confused for a minute. Then her deep black eyes cleared and a sly sparkle lit them. "Yes, dear.

That is a very good idea and actually I was planning that for your Special ceremony — a promotion of sorts."

"Oh, Mum, this will be great. I can't wait to tell him."

"Don't!" she squawked. "It's to be a surprise. No one is supposed to know until the minute it happens. You keep your beak shut!"

"Oh, yes, Mum. I will," he said.

"I mean it, Nyroc. One peep out of you and the ceremony is canceled."

"Madam, I don't mean to interrupt this important discussion with your son, but I have changed my mind," Gwyndor said.

"Changed your mind? Changed your mind about what?"

"I shall stay on and make the fire claws," Gwyndor said. As he spoke he flipped his head about so he would not have to look directly into Nyra's eyes.

"We deeply appreciate this, Gwyndor," she said. "What, might I ask, accounts for this change of mind?"

"I don't know, madam." He paused. "Sometimes one just feels that one must do something and is not sure why."

"I'll tell you why you changed your mind. You did it because you knew it was the right thing to do."

Gwyndor blinked and then replied, "Yes, I think perhaps you could say that. It is the right thing to do." When he spoke these words he was not looking at Nyra but at her son, Nyroc. He was staying for the hatchling's sake and yet he did not know why. "But I must tell you, madam, I shall have to fly off for a brief time before I start the claws. I must collect the right metals and the right embers for this job. It requires special materials." Even saying the word "special" made a shiver run through Gwyndor's gizzard.

It was a lie of course. Gwyndor had all the materials he needed with him. His intention was to contact the nearest slipgizzle and find out all he could about this Special ceremony. Slipgizzles were the secret agents that informed the Guardians of Ga'Hoole of the doings in other kingdoms. Many Rogue smiths also happened to be slipgizzles. The fact was that Rogue smiths were known for being mavericks, slightly eccentric, usually without family ties, and not attached to any particular group — few gave out their true names. But Gwyndor had been raised in a very traditional family and was familiar with all of the customs and ceremonies of owl families and communities. Yet he had never in all his life and wanderings encountered anything called the Special ceremony. It worried him and he felt it was urgent that he learn more about the ceremony planned for Nyroc, which the Pure Ones kept shrouded in such secrecy. Therefore, he had decided to go to the nearest slipgizzle he could find. He had heard there was a new Rogue smith somewhere between the Shadow Forest and the Barrens. He would go search for that smith. He hoped the smith might be a slipgizzle. Slipgizzles knew just about everything. So one of them might know what this Special ceremony was all about.

As the grays of twilight gathered on the evening of that same day, Nyroc saw Gwyndor packing his kit to leave. "I thought you had already left," Nyroc said as he lighted down on the ledge.

"Naw, too many crows around to fly off until it really gets dark."

"I've heard about crows," Nyroc said.

"And I'll wager that everything you've heard about them is true. A frinkin' awful lot they are. You don't want to be caught out alone in daylight, believe me. There'll be a mob of them on you 'fore you can cry 'Glaux help!'"

Nyroc was looking at the tools of Gwyndor's trade. This Masked Owl, who could draw fire from a bucket and twist metal into odd shapes with his hammer and tongs, fascinated him. He peered now into the glowering bucket of coals.

"You like my little fellows in there, do you, lad?" Gwyndor said.

"Yes, I guess so." Even though the coals had not ignited into flames, to Nyroc they seemed to breathe like living things and like living things they had stories, the shapes of which he could almost see deep within their radiant glow. When he had told his mother that he had been thinking about the color green, he had actually been thinking about the images he had glimpsed in the flames at the Marking and the story he felt the flames would reveal if he dared to look again. And yet there was a compulsion growing in Nyroc to know this story. *The truth!* Yes, he felt that this truth had something to do with his terrible uncle Soren. But he could not be sure. And then again what could be worse or more frightening than what the bones of a split spine had already revealed — the murderous rampage of Soren that had killed his father?

Once again, Gwyndor regarded him. A strange feeling tingled in the Masked Owl's gizzard. *What does this young'un see even now in the coals that have not yet sparked into flames?*

# CHAPTER SIX

# Murder with a Cute Name

Gwyndor rose over the burnt land, spiraling higher and higher. The Rogue smith, the best slipgizzle he knew, had once lived in Silverveil and even forged some battle claws for the Pure Ones, but rumor had it that one of their lieutenants had roughed her up and she had left Silverveil and gone somewhere near the border of the Shadow Forest and the Barrens. But where? He would have to rely on his instincts. And Rogue smiths had very good instincts concerning where their fellow smiths might set up shop. There were certain kinds of landscape that suited them better than others. They liked caves, for one thing, caves in old-growth forests that grew close to new-growth ones. The new-growth forests provided them with brush and tinder for their fires. But the old-growth forests with their widely spaced trees allowed the smoke from their fires to clear out more quickly.

Rogue smiths liked the ruins of old castles and churches from the time of the Others in particular. The Rogue smith of Silverveil had set up in a prime spot when she had worked there. He wondered if someone else had taken it over. It wasn't that much out of his way to fly there and take a look. Glaux, if no one had claimed the spot he might set up there himself once he left the Pure Ones for good — which couldn't be soon enough. The higher he flew and the farther away he went, the better he felt. But something had gotten to him about that little hatchling — Nyroc. He knew he had to come back before that Special ceremony took place. But he would be useless if he came back without knowing what it was about. He hoped he could find out. He supposed if he couldn't find the Rogue smith he was looking for he could fly back to Ambala and seek out Mist again. She might know. But the winds this time of year were not favorable for flying to Ambala. It would take too much time beating against those easterlies.

By the time the constellation of the Golden Talons was rising in the eastern sky, Gwyndor was flying over Silverveil on a direct course for the old ruins where the Rogue smith had once set up her shop. "By Glaux!" the Masked Owl muttered as he saw tendrils of smoke rising in the night. "Someone has already claimed it!" Then as if to confirm the fact, he heard the sound of hammer on anvil ringing out into the night.

He began a banking turn as he prepared to fly in. The

forge was going full blast, and he could see the owl busily at work with hammer and tongs. It was not good to interrupt a smith in the midst of work. It could even be dangerous. So Gwyndor lighted down on a stone wall that had once enclosed a walled rose garden and waited patiently until the smith turned from the work.

The smith was making what looked like a rather elaborate decorative piece of some sort. Gwyndor supposed that since the defeat of the Pure Ones, there had not been much call for battle claws. He watched as the smith dipped the red-hot piece into a stone basin of water and then turned around. The Masked Owl blinked in amazement. It was she — the old Rogue smith of the Silverveil.

"Thought someone was here," she said. The Snowy Owl's pure white plumage was sooty with ash.

"You came back!" Gwyndor exclaimed.

"So I did. It's the best place for a smithy in the Southern Kingdoms. I didn't want to give it up because of those bullies. Only the ragtag ends of them left now, and I understand they are down in the canyonlands somewhere."

"That they are," Gwyndor replied. The Snowy looked up with interest.

"You say that as if you know for sure."

"I do. That's why I'm here."

"Don't ask me to make anything for them numbskull owls. The war's over. I'm finished with war, as a matter of fact. I'm into" — she paused for dramatic effect — "more artistic things." She held the tongs up in the air. There was an oddly twisted thing pinched between the two parts of the tongs.

"What's that?"

"It's free-form, abstract. You know, I come from a very artistic family." Gwyndor had heard something of this. It was said that this Snowy's sister was the famous singer of the Great Ga'Hoole Tree.

"What does it do?"

"It pleases me," the Snowy said simply.

"It pleases you?"

"That's reason enough to make something. Not everything has to be useful."

"Yes, I suppose so," Gwyndor replied, but he had not come here to be lectured by an artistic blacksmith. "Look, the reason I came — well, it's hard to explain."

"Start by explaining why you were mucking around with those frinkin' owls."

Gwyndor was relieved. This sounded like the old Rogue smith he knew. She was known for her salty language. So

Gwyndor explained as best he could and when he finished the Snowy stared at him for several seconds before speaking.

"Let me get this straight — you went there because you felt that Mist somehow sent you, without ever saying to do it?" Gwyndor nodded. The Snowy continued. "She has a way of doing that, I know. And you say you think this hatchling might have fire sight, could be a flame reader?" Again Gwyndor nodded. "Well, my friend, other than Orf, there hasn't been a flame reader in more than one hundred years. They are extremely rare. But go on. You haven't gotten to your very important question."

"Yes," Gwyndor sighed. "You see, this little fellow . . . They call him Nyroc."

"Figures," the Snowy said disdainfully. "Mum's name is Nyra, right?"

"Yes. And let's hope this one doesn't grow up to be like his mum — or his da. But as I was saying, Nyroc has gone through all the usual ceremonies a young owlet has to do by now. Just had his First Prey ceremony. He got himself a nice plump little chipmunk."

"Never cared for them myself," the Snowy said. "They give me gas."

"Well, the next ceremony is one I have never heard of."

"What do you mean, never heard of? The next

ceremony after First Prey should be First Moss. That's always a fun one — going out looking for all the softest mosses for the hollow."

"Well, there's no moss now in the canyonlands. So maybe they have to substitute something. I don't know."

"What do they call it?" she asked.

"The Special ceremony," Gwyndor answered.

The Snowy suddenly wilfed and seemed to shrink to half her size. She dropped her tongs. "No!" she gasped.

When the Snowy had recovered herself, she turned to Gwyndor. "Come into my hollow. I have some honey mead. Good for a chilly night. And I'll try to explain."

Gwyndor followed the Snowy through a passageway in the stone wall to what had been a courtyard of some sort, and then down steps into a cellar. "This is very nice," Gwyndor said, looking around.

"I think it was a wine cellar. I make my nest in that barrel over there. Quite sweet-smelling. Care for some vole with the honey mead?" the Rogue smith offered.

"Sure."

As they ate, the Snowy looked at Gwyndor darkly and began to explain. "I've heard bad things. Very bad things, indeed! I have heard that to become a true member of the Pure Ones, an officer, one must kill something. And not in battle." The Snowy's voice dwindled off.

A quiver ran through Gwyndor's gizzard. "You mean to kill without hunger? To kill for no reason?"

"I am not talking about hunting for food. I'm talking about murder."

"Murder!" Gwyndor whispered. "You mean they kill one of our own kind?"

"Yes. They say that Soren was to be Kludd's Special years ago. Before he was a Pure One, he shoved Soren out of the nest, thinking that the fall would kill him. Or at least that a ground predator would get him. Kludd hadn't counted on a St. Aggie's patrol picking Soren up."

"You can't mean he was actually going to murder his own brother?"

"That's exactly what I mean and they don't call it 'murder,' of course. No, this ceremony is called Tupsi."

"Tupsi — what in Glaux's name does that mean?"

"Something like Tytonic Union Pure Special Initiation — Tupsi for short. Murder with a cute name."

"This is monstrous! I must tell the young'un immediately." Gwyndor stopped drinking the honey mead from the metal flagon the Snowy had set before him.

"I am not sure if that is such a good idea," the Snowy Owl replied cryptically.

"What in Glaux's name do you mean — not a good idea? What am I supposed to do? Stand by and let this thuggish bunch of owls turn a fine young'un into a worse brute than his father?"

"These lessons are perhaps best learned on one's own."

Gwyndor blinked. "I don't see why."

Then even more cryptically, the Snowy Rogue smith said, "Truth must be revealed and not simply told."

*This Snowy is just plain yoicks!* Gwyndor thought. And he had no intention of withholding from Nyroc the horrific truth about Tupsi.

# CHAPTER SEVEN

## *Hammer and Tongs!*

M*urder with a cute name! Murder with any name is still murder. Tupsi!*

That was all Gwyndor could think of as he flew back to the canyonlands the following evening in the first snowfall of the season.

Normally, Gwyndor would have loved being out on a night like this. The moon was barely newing. Only a sliver of light hung up there in the dark sky, behind the moving snow clouds. Big fluffy snowflakes drifted slowly against the dark blue-gray of night. He loved it when snowflakes fell slowly, spinning, turning to a music all their own. But there was no music in this night for Gwyndor. There was just the one thought: He had to get back and somehow save young Nyroc from this terrible thing called Tupsi. There was a prisoner called Smutty who the Pure Ones were holding. He was accused of cowardice during the battle they called The Burning. He had heard some talk that the charges were questionable. He hadn't thought much of it because he knew that Sooties, particularly Lesser Sooties, were held in low esteem and the first to be accused of anything in the Union. Was it this Sooty named Smutty who would be the victim in this brutal ceremony? And were they really planning on turning Nyroc, a perfect young hatchling who performed every task put to him so flawlessly, into Smutty's murderer? And would he become the perfect murderer? The flawless executioner? And coupled with what Gwyndor suspected to be Nyroc's extraordinary capacity for flame reading would this not become a deadly combination? Gwyndor felt a tremendous shudder pass through his gizzard. *Great Glaux, he would be a hundred times worse than his father, Kludd!*

And what exactly was he, Gwyndor, supposed to do about it? He was tempted to turn back, head to Ambala, and find Mist to ask for some instructions. But Mist was strange. She didn't give instructions.

The easterly wind had suddenly backed around to south and then southwest.

"Oh, Glaux! What's that wind doing?" Gwyndor felt himself losing speed. If this was a real headwind, he would be ramming into it for the next few hours and would never get to the canyonlands before dawn. And he had to! He had no choice but to go on. If Nyroc did have fire sight, if he was a flame reader, and if he in fact had perceived glimpses of the great Ember of Hoole with the blue flame in its ruby-red heart, then he must not under any circumstances be allowed to go through with the murderous initiation ceremony of the Pure Ones. That a natural flame reader would be trained to murder was unthinkable. Such a power turned to evil would endanger the future of the owl universe. The ceremony must be stopped. But would Gwyndor himself be forced to murder to stop it? The very thought was enough to make one go yeep.

Gwyndor took a deep breath and somehow found new strength. He carved a turn and headed southwest toward the Great Horns of the canyonlands, battling the ever-increasing headwind. His flight had slowed, and the black was leaking out of the night. Soon it would be dawn. No time for a lone owl to be abroad. But even as he grew more and more weary in his mind, in his gizzard he felt that he must risk daylight flying. There was no choice. So on he flew.

The morning star was just above the horizon when he heard the first wing beats behind him. *Crows!* He felt his gizzard grow still. *I am going yeep!* he thought, and the Masked Owl began to plummet. But then something happened. His gizzard seemed to explode with sudden fury. He pulled out of his plunging spiral and flew downwind. He twisted his head to see how far behind they were.

Not far enough! The odds weren't good — three crows to one owl. But he was a better flier than any crow. He forgot his tired wings. He felt a new energy flow through him.

He was flying heavy with his kit. Why not let it drop? But then he would lose the coals, the really choice ones the Rogue smith of Silverveil had given him. He had another idea. There was not much time and the maneuver would take some doing, but if soldier owls could fight with battle claws and flaming branches, why couldn't he fight with the tools of his trade?

He spotted a ledge ahead. He quickly landed on the ledge, set down his precious bucket of coals, and took out his hammer and tongs. The three crows were almost on him when he flew into them straight from the ledge, swinging his hammer and wielding the tongs, which held a hot coal. He poked one of the crows in the primaries of its left wing. The bird cawed and the smell of fried feathers whirled through the air. But the other two were still coming after him. He felt something hit him in his tail feathers. He began to wobble. With his tail damaged he could hardly keep his flight steady. This was bad. Drops of blood splattered the dawn. Was it his blood? No time to worry.

He wheeled around still swinging his hammer in one talon and gripping the tongs with the hot burning coal in the other. The crow with the singed wing was back.

*Impossible!* There was a sudden downdraft that sucked all four birds into a trough of still air. Just beneath him was the black back of a crow. It glistened like a polished anvil. With all his might he struck that feathered anvil with his hammer. The crow broke in half like a dried twig. The other two let out terrible caws that ripped the stillness of the dawn.

Then as fast as they had come, they were gone. Gwyndor was exhausted. He felt himself losing altitude. *I have to go on. I have to go on. I must get to Nyroc before it's too late.*

And the dawn bled into day, and the day became the night, and the night was thick with shadows and dreams. The crows became hagsfiends like dark vapors flying through the night. Gwyndor moaned in pain and fear.

# CHAPTER EIGHT
## Facts of Life and Death

"Do you know what scrooms are, my little hatchling?" Nyra asked her son.

"Sort of. But, Mum, I am an expert flier now and I have killed my first prey. Do you have to keep calling me a hatchling? I've been through my First Flight ceremony."

"Well, yes, that's true. But we still have Tupsi, the Special ceremony. And after that, I shall truly no longer be able to get away with calling you 'hatchling.'" She churred softly. "Nor even owlet. For you shall be a soldier after the Special ceremony that we call Tupsi."

"Tupsi, I like the sound of that," Nyroc said.

"It stands for Tytonic Union of Pure Ones Special Initiation."

"But what is the special initiation? I wish I knew more about it. What am I supposed to do?"

"Tonight I shall tell you more about it. And more about your history, and about scrooms, too."

And so she began.

"A scroom, my dear, is a spirit that cannot rest until its work on Earth is finished." Nyra blinked. Her dark eyes as polished as river stones seemed to look into another place, another time, another night. There was something spooky about his mum, Nyroc suddenly realized. For the first time he was afraid of her in a new way — not because he had done something less than perfectly or asked a question that he should not have asked. This was different. She seemed to have gone into some sort of a trance. She began to speak in a scratchy singsong voice.

> There were three scrooms who came to me
> And said Nyroc shall be king
> And with this Special ceremony
> His glory shall long and loudly ring.

Nyroc's eyes brightened. "You mean, Mum, that I am really to be king, supreme commander like my great father?"

"You will. Once you have completed the Special ceremony."

"But what is it?"

"The Special ceremony is a sacrifice of sorts. But it is also more. It is a courageous act — a blood act."

"A blood act? Sacrifice?"

54

"Sacrifice is giving up something that is difficult to give up. Something you care for."

"I get it! It's like killing something you might want to eat but then not eating it, right?"

Nyra's eyes glittered. "Not exactly, but close. I shall explain more as we draw nearer to the time of the ceremony."

*Centipedes?* Nyroc wondered. He *loved* centipedes. They were one of his favorite foods. But he had a feeling that it was not centipedes. Centipedes, after all, didn't have blood. Perhaps a fox, or something larger. *Could it be the prisoner he was to kill?* He did not want to, would not, think about that.

Maybe it had to do with his da's battle claws. Yes, that must be it. He would be required to kill something with his da's battle claws! His mum had saved them for him. They were pretty special, and so was his da's mask, which hung in their hollow in the cliff. Actually, Nyroc thought, the mask gave him the creeps. Every time he looked at it he wilfed a bit. But he was drawn to the battle claws. They were his inspiration. Everything he had learned how to do was because of the claws. They burnished his ambition and stirred his gizzard every time he was put to a new challenge. *You shall grow into those claws, Nyroc, his mother had told him. . . . You were born to wear them into battle. Regard them closely, my hatchling.*

Indeed, no one knew how closely he had studied them and yearned for their power with the deepest part of his gizzard.

"But first," Nyra continued, "you must learn to hate." She regarded her son closely as she said this.

"Hate — why hate?"

"My dear, hate can make you strong. Very strong."

"But I don't hate anything."

"Give it time, my little hatchling," she said. "I shall help you learn to hate. These are the facts of life and death, my dear."

Nyroc felt as if his gizzard were cracking with fear. He knew he was wilfing in front of his mother's eyes. He was trying to be brave. He tried to summon the image of his father's battle claws. "You will help me?"

"Of course. I'm your mother. What are mothers for but to teach their little ones?"

"To hate?"

Nyra nodded. "And here is your first lesson. You know who Soren is."

"My uncle," Nyroc answered. "The owl who killed my father."

"Well, it's as easy as that."

Nyroc's eyes shined now. "You mean I am supposed to hate him?" he replied excitedly.

"Exactly."

"Well, that's not hard, Mum. I already do." And in Nyroc's mind's eye an image blazed: his father's battle claws on his own talons tearing through the backbone of Soren. He could hear the crack of the bones, could see the blood. Nyra watched her son and observed how his black eyes grew blacker and harder just as his father's once had. *Killer eyes!* The likeness to his father almost took her breath away.

"You see," Nyra finally spoke, "hate comes easily. There will, however, be harder lessons."

But this did not concern Nyroc. This first lesson had been easy. It was natural to hate his father's killer. He felt his gizzard stir with a heat he had never before known. *So this is hate*, he thought with great wonder. It was a most powerful emotion. If this was what his mum meant by hate, how hard could the other lessons be?

"Yes," said Nyra. "You must learn to hate him. You must think of your da's broken spine every time you hear Soren's name, every time you hear the words 'Guardians of Ga'Hoole.'"

"Yes, Mum, yes. I shall hate. I promise."

"Swear upon the battle claws of your father," Nyra whispered.

Nyroc hopped over to where the claws hung on the

stone wall and raised one talon. "On these claws of my great father, I do swear to hate."

"And to kill," his mother added softly.

"And to kill," Nyroc repeated, and once more his eyes turned black and hard. Like black diamonds with a fierce sparkle at their very center.

Nyra peered out of the hollow and saw the last scraps of the night dissolving into the gray of the new day. "It is nearing twixt time. Go to sleep now, my little hatchling. I am proud of you. Know that." But deep in Nyra's gizzard there was a tremor of doubt. She did not know why. It made no sense. She had seen the dark glitter in those eyes so like Kludd's. He was her perfect hatchling and yet she thought, *There is something too sweet in this lad's gizzard, something too sweet. If I could only drain that sweetness from his gizzard and replace it with the gallgrot of his father. But his eyes. His eyes are killer eyes — are they not?*

# CHAPTER NINE

# *Burrowing Owls to the Rescue*

T he family of Burrowing Owls looked at the Rogue smith who had tumbled out of the sky with his bucket of coals, tongs, and hammer. Kalo, their daughter, entered the burrow. Her father asked, "Did you find the last coal?"

"I think so, Da. It was under the edge of that boulder."

Burrowing Owls were known for their walking abilities. Their long, featherless legs and their talons were extremely strong. They dug holes to live in, much preferring a ground hollow to one in a tree.

"Well, he'll be pleased with that when he wakes up," her father replied.

"I hope it's soon," said Kalo. "He's moaning like he's having the worst daymares ever."

"Screaming about scrooms and crows," her mother added. "Crows are what got him, I think. They always go for the tail feathers first."

"And to think he was being attacked in the sky right above us and we didn't even know it," the father said for the third time.

"Harry" — his mate, Myrtle, looked at him — "what could we have done, really? We have no idea how many crows there were. They could have outnumbered us and then we would all have been finished."

"But maybe they wouldn't have outnumbered us," Harry said. "See, this is what comes of living underground."

Harry, the father of this brood, was a bit of an eccentric. For some time, he had been trying to persuade his family to have at least a summer home in a tree someplace.

"Harry, we've gone through this a million times," his mate said.

"Myrtle," he said.

She knew what was coming.

"Need I remind you," he went on, "that myrtle is a plant that grows on a tree? You'd be a natural."

Myrtle blinked. "Harry, somewhere out there, there's a Barn Owl whose name is Dirtle, just plain Dirt for short. Do you think her mate is trying to persuade her to set up housekeeping in a burrow?"

"And besides," Kalo said, "I don't want to be the only Burrowing Owl living in a tree. What would my friends think? It's just too weird."

The family continued their good-natured bickering, not noticing that Gwyndor had begun to stir.

"Where am I?" Gwyndor said in a low, rasping voice.

"My goodness! He's awake!" Myrtle gasped.

"Sir." Harry stepped forward. "You are in our burrow. You seemed to have fallen out of the sky."

"My coals! My coals!" Gwyndor cried hoarsely.

"Don't worry." Myrtle bent down to speak to him. "Our daughter, Kalo, fetched them all — at least we think she found them all."

"How many did she find?"

"Nine, sir." Kalo had stepped up next to her mother. "And your hammer and tongs and the bucket," she added.

Gwyndor sank back on the soft bed of rabbit fur with great relief.

"Were you mobbed, sir?" Harry asked.

"Yes," Gwyndor replied. "There were three of them."

"Three against one!" Myrtle said, her voice hushed with awe. "And you survived!"

"I survived, no doubt thanks to you."

"Your wounds don't look too bad. We'll just send our daughter out for some fresh worms to put on them," Harry said, and then with some emphasis added, "Nest-maid snakes are hard to come by here. They prefer trees, I guess." He spun his head toward his mate.

"Drop it, Harry! Our daughter is just as good as any nest-maid snake at digging up worms."

"I must be on my way immediately," Gwyndor said, struggling up from the rabbit fur. He had forgotten how very good Burrowing Owls were at rabbit hunting with their finely honed talons, and how they lined their nests with the soft fur. *Lovely practice*, Gwyndor thought.

"You're going? You can't be serious, sir," Harry said.

"Oh, but I am. It is essential that I get to my destination as soon as possible."

The entire family of Burrowing Owls blinked in astonishment as Gwyndor staggered to his feet, then reached for his kit. "I cannot thank you enough. I shall never forget your kindness."

"But, sir," Harry interrupted.

"No, I must go — without delay. Good-bye and Glaux bless."

A few seconds later, they heard the flutter of his wings as Gwyndor took off.

# CHAPTER TEN

# *One Wing Beat at a Time*

The contrary winds had eased up, making flying less difficult. As the Great Horns came into sight, Gwyndor at last allowed himself to feel his fatigue. He ran over his plan in his head. He had to get Nyroc alone. He would ask Nyra if her young son could help him set up the forge for the fire claws. He would say that as a Rogue smith, he had a sense about which young'uns would make good blacksmiths and he thought that perhaps Nyroc might be one. He felt this would be an irresistible idea for Nyra. If the Pure Ones had their own smith they would have an endless supply of weapons.

*And then what?* Gwyndor thought. How was one supposed to go about telling a young owlet, a near-hatchling, that he was going to be asked to kill another owl in cold blood? And after that, what? There were many parts of Gwyndor's plan that were not worked out. But he would just have to take it one wing beat at a time, as his dear old mum used to say. The words of the Snowy still haunted him: *These lessons are perhaps best learned on one's own.*

"Nonsense!" Gwyndor muttered to himself. First, he would have to find a spot to set up his forge. The making of the fire claws was actually a ruse so it did not matter much where he set up. A plan began to fall into place. As soon as he told Nyroc the true meaning of the Special ceremony he would have to leave — leave or be killed. If Nyroc wanted to leave with him, he could. Gwyndor didn't much like company, but he could point Nyroc in the right direction, suggest some region where he might find a safe hollow to hide in. But then again, even at this young age Nyroc looked a great deal like his mum. He would immediately be identified as one of the Pure Ones, who were welcome nowhere.

Suddenly, a call cracked the air. "Hail, the Rogue smith has returned!" It was one of the lookouts from the watch perch on the Great Horns. Gwyndor spiraled down toward the Pure Ones' outpost in the canyonlands.

He saw some owls, Nyra among them, come out from their stone hollows and gather on a ledge.

As he lighted down, Gwyndor looked for Nyroc. Was he too late? Had the ceremony already happened? He then spotted Nyroc on a ledge looking quite fit. Even elated. He must have once again performed some task flawlessly.

"Welcome, sir." Nyra nodded to the Rogue smith. "I trust you've brought the proper tools for making our fire claws."

"Yes, madam. I need only now to find the right place to set up my forge." He cast a glance toward Nyroc. "Madam, if I might proffer a suggestion?"

"Yes?" Nyra said.

"I would like some help in the setting up of my forge."

"Of course." She turned to her first lieutenant. "Uglamore?"

"Oh, madam, that is very kind of you," Gwyndor hastened to say, "but I was wondering . . ."

"Yes?" she snapped. Owls seldom questioned Nyra's choices.

"I was wondering if your son, Nyroc, might assist me."

"Nyroc? Why Nyroc?" she asked Gwyndor.

"Because, madam, I think he has the gift for fire." This was truer than anyone there, except Gwyndor, could possibly know. If Nyroc truly was a flame reader, his powers went far beyond those of a blacksmith.

"You think he could learn to be a smith?"

"Absolutely, madam, and a very fine smith at that. He may be born to command — eventually — but could he not in the meantime learn, and then teach, smithing?"

There was a stirring among the owls. "Well, this is

indeed an unexpected idea, and perhaps a blessing, if what you say is true."

"I am seldom wrong about such things. Yes, madam, if he has the gift, I could train him — and he in turn could train others — other Pure Ones — to make all the battle claws and fire claws you will ever need."

Nyra's eyes shone. She ruffled her feathers, and her face seemed to grow even larger. "Come forward, Nyroc." The other owls parted on the ledge to make a path for the young owl. "Did you hear what the Rogue smith said?"

"Yes, General Mam," he said.

"You could start your apprenticeship directly following your Special ceremony."

"And when is that to be, madam?" Gwyndor asked, trying to keep the alarm out of his voice.

"Tomorrow evening."

"That is unfortunate," he said.

"What is the problem?" Nyra asked.

"It is essential that I find a place for my forge and get my fires going immediately. I have brought special coals. The first step of a young apprentice's education is to see what kind of place makes for a good forge and the setting of the coals."

"Oh, I see. Well, no harm in him accompanying you now."

"Good," Gwyndor said. At last he would have the chance to speak to Nyroc alone. It had been worth everything: the contrary winds, the mobbing by crows. *Yes, one wing beat at a time — one wing beat at a time,* his mum's wise words echoed in his head.

# CHAPTER ELEVEN

## Free Will

Nyroc was overjoyed by Gwyndor's words. *Who would have ever thought that the Rogue smith would invite me to be an apprentice? He says I have the gift, the gift of fire. I'm not sure what that means.* Nyroc was thinking all this as he and Gwyndor flew over a ridge on the far side of the Great Horns. They had been flying for a while before Gwyndor finally began his descent. Much to Nyroc's surprise, the Rogue smith settled on a ledge high above the ground. There were no caves in sight.

"A ledge seems an odd place for a forge," Nyroc said.

Gwyndor was about to blurt everything out, to say, "Nyroc, I didn't bring you here to make a forge. We shall not be making any forges." But once again, the Snowy Owl's words coursed through him: *Truth must be revealed and not simply told.* Perhaps he could build a fire and see what it revealed to the young'un. If the Snowy Owl was right, the truth might be stronger coming from the fire, might go deeper — right to the center of Nyroc's gizzard. "You're right," Gwyndor replied quickly. "This is no place for a forge. I just need a bit of a rest. It was a hard trip back. Headwinds, you know."

Nyroc looked at him. He wasn't sure why they had stopped on the ledge. It had seemed at first as if the old Rogue smith was about to say something to him, something important. He was a curious, almost funny-looking old owl, Nyroc thought. Relative of the Barn Owl with the same almost heart-shaped facial disk except that instead of being pure white, a shadowy mask stretched across it. His beak had permanent dark smudges from a lifetime spent tending a forge. Nearly all of his leg feathers had been scorched off and his thin knobby knees poked through the remaining feathery bits. His talons were rough and blackened from working with the hammer and tongs. But now Gwyndor spread his wings and lifted into flight and Nyroc followed. Soon they found the perfect place for a forge. It was a cave in the base of a cliff with a good dirt floor. Gwyndor began to tear at the dirt with his talons, hollowing out a shallow pit. From his kit, he removed some twigs for kindling, then drew out coals that were still red-hot. Nyroc felt a stir in his gizzard as the first flames leaped up from the kindling. "Step closer, lad," Gwyndor instructed.

Nyroc moved closer. He stood very still. He did not feel the heat. He peered deeply into the flames. The flames danced into shapes again, telling, revealing shapes that were disturbingly strange and familiar. Gwyndor watched him intently. He saw the young owl's eyes glaze over. *Look at it, lad, look deeply. Now is the time to be brave. Don't deny what the fire reveals.* But Gwyndor kept his beak clamped shut. Oh, how he wanted to tell Nyroc what horror lay ahead but he knew in the deepest part of his gizzard that the Rogue smith of Silverveil was right. Nyroc must learn this lesson on his own.

The world began to spin for Nyroc. A pellet flew out of his beak. Then another. He was yarping in distress.

"Steady, lad. Steady," Gwyndor said. He extended his wing and touched Nyroc's back.

"Why did you really bring me here?" Nyroc demanded. "What is this about?" the young owl asked in a tremulous voice.

"I can't tell you."

"Why not?"

"It is all there in the fire for you to find."

Nyroc forced himself to look back at the fire. Gwyndor wanted to tell him to look deeper. To not be afraid. But he himself was afraid for the lad.

Finally, Nyroc backed away from the fire. The young hatchling had suddenly aged. He looked coldly at Gwyndor. "I saw things," he whispered. "I saw things I do not understand. I saw things I cannot believe . . . about my parents, about the Pure Ones."

Gwyndor desperately wanted to ask if he had seen the truth about the Special ceremony, but he resisted.

"Why do I see these things?" he asked Gwyndor.

"I don't know why."

"But are they true?"

"I cannot tell you."

"Cannot or will not?"

"Will not," Gwyndor replied reluctantly. "Because, Nyroc, if I tell you, you will not truly believe. Belief is found in one's self, in one's gizzard, in one's heart, in one's mind. It has no power if it is simply ordered like a command."

These words made Nyroc blink.

"But why would the Pure Ones do what I see in these flames?"

"I can't answer that except to say that the Pure Ones have very strange ideas." The Rogue smith's voice dwindled to a whisper.

"Strange ideas about what? What do you mean?"

"Ideas about what makes a courageous owl, ideas about power." Gwyndor shook his head in frustration. "I cannot explain it. I hardly understand it myself." The silence between them was thick as each retreated into deep, gizzard-stirring reflections. Gwyndor suddenly had a notion. He could say something. Something that might help the poor owl without really telling him the truth outright. He wondered if Nyroc knew much about St. Aggie's Academy. "Lad, have you heard about St. Aggie's?"

"Oh, yes, we conquered them long before my hatching. Their place was rich in flecks."

"Well, there was more," Gwyndor said. "There was a place called the glaucidium where the young owlets were moon blinked."

"Moon blinked?" Nyroc asked. "What's that?"

So Gwyndor explained about St. Aggie's, a cruel institution despite its claim of being a refuge for orphans. "It was in the glaucidium that the young orphan owls were forced to sleep-march under the blazing light of the moon. It broke their will and made them docile creatures totally under the power of St. Aggie's leaders. They could not think. They could not make any decision on their own. They had no will — no free will."

"Free will," Nyroc murmured the two words softly. *But what does all this have to do with me? Or the Pure Ones? Or my parents? It all happened when the St. Aggie's owls were in power. It was over when the Pure Ones conquered them.*

Gwyndor drew the young owl close to him. The shadows of the early evening mingled with the dark patches of the Masked Owl's face. His beak was blacker than Nyroc had first thought and was a bit twisted. "It has everything to do with you, lad. You see, Nyroc, you have free will! You can think things through, consult your own gizzard, do what *you* think is right. You can be what you want to be."

*Be what I want to be . . .* The words rang ominously in his head. He felt his gizzard grow very still.

"But I only want to be the best, most perfect Pure One ever," he said. "I must grow into my father's battle claws. I must bring these claws great honor."

His words echoed hollowly in the cave and as hard as he tried to summon the great enthralling image of the burnished battle claws, he could not. The claws seemed to grow dim, to dissolve like mere mist into a deepening fog. He looked back into the fire for a long time, then he wilfed and grew slender as a fragile branch.

"What do you see, lad, what do you see?" Gwyndor whispered.

Nyroc turned from the fire. "Nothing."

Gwyndor knew that the young owl was not telling the truth. Nyroc had seen something in those flames, something so awful that he could not believe it. And he was denying it not only to Gwyndor, but to himself. The Masked Owl was feeling desperate.

"Nyroc, there isn't much time."

But Nyroc turned his back, hopped to the cave's entrance, spread his wings, and lifted himself into the sky. From the cave mouth Gwyndor watched the young owl carve a slow circle above and head back to the stone hollow he shared with his mum, Nyra.

Nyra and Nyroc had been flying their normal rounds on their evening flight through the canyonlands. Tonight, however, Nyra noticed that her son was unusually quiet and distracted.

"Is something troubling you, my dear?"

"No, Mum, nothing. Nothing at all."

They were flying over the jagged narrow canyons that had once been occupied by the owls of St. Aggie's. Nyroc looked down. "Is that where the glaucidium was, Mum?"

"Why, yes, how do you know about that?"

"Just do. You know, talk and things."

A nervous twinge tweaked Nyra's gizzard. "What did you hear?"

"Something about how they moon blinked the orphan owls so that they couldn't think."

"Probably couldn't think to begin with," she said dismissively. "Very few Barn Owls among them."

"Hmmm," Nyroc said.

Nyra looked at him suspiciously.

"Mum, tell me once more about the night my da was killed."

"Of course, dear. It was in the Battle of The Burning. We had all been brutally attacked by the owls of Ga'Hoole. They outnumbered us and had more weapons, although we were much superior in our firefighting. Nonetheless, your father fought on bravely. He and a small contingent of owls had been chasing some of the fiercest of the Ga'Hoolian warriors when they were suddenly forced into a cave by the backdraft of the fire. They didn't know that a larger band of Ga'Hoolian owls was already in this cave and they were caught completely by surprise. In a maddened frenzy, Soren flew directly at your father and sliced his back through the spine with an ice sword. It happened so quickly, there was no time for any of the Pure Ones to . . . to . . ." She was searching for the word.

"Think?" Nyroc asked.

Nyra gave him a poisonous look. She did not like the way this conversation was going. Not at all.

"There was no time for orders to be issued and obeyed," she said coolly.

*Can a soldier only act when a command is given? Can soldiers never think or act on their own?* Nyroc thought. However, he knew better than to ask such questions. And, in fact, he did not need to ask. What he had seen in the flames of the fire was nothing at all like what his mother had just described. Either the flames were lying or his mother was. It was time for him to find out the truth.

# CHAPTER TWELVE
## Blood in the Flames

The night had thinned into the dawn. Mist pearled the charred landscape below as Nyroc flew to the hollow in the cleft of the rock wall. He alighted on the ledge outside. What he had seen in the fire was unbelievable, some of it so unbelievable that the images within the flames had made no sense at all. Well, he must find out for himself. It was the only way. He knew Gwyndor was right about this.

He stepped into the hollow. His mum had fluffed up the lichen she used instead of moss for his bedding and plucked some fresh down from her own breast. Nyra was sleeping soundly in her corner. He looked at the tufts of down, then at his mother. He remembered the first time he had ever seen her pull out tuft after tuft from beneath her breast feathers. It had amazed him.

"Doesn't that hurt?" he had asked as he watched her.

"Not when you do it for your dear hatchling," she had replied.

And Nyroc knew that because he had no father and

this burnt land no longer had the soft moss used in nests, his mum had to pluck twice as much of her own down. He had wondered if he could ever do such a thing. He didn't like pain and could not imagine that it would be any less painful if you were doing it for someone you loved. He had complained bitterly when his first flight feathers had begun to bud. The shaft points of the primaries hurt as they poked through his tender skin.

He wanted to whisper out to her now, *Mum, what I saw in the fire — this isn't true.* The first time he had looked through the flames, at the Marking ceremony in the cave where his father had died, he had seen a place he did not recognize, a strange landscape where weird creatures with four legs and strangely colored eyes loped through swirling mists and vapors. And then there had been the curious thing like a flame made of stone, orange in color with the lick of deep blue at its center, and between the inner blue and the outer orange what he thought might be the color green. This reminded Nyroc that his mum had promised to take him to see a tree after the Special ceremony if he performed it well. Nyroc's gizzard gave a sickening twist. A darkness seemed to flood through it as it did every time he thought of the Special ceremony. He quickly pushed all thoughts of it from his mind.

He remembered instead how oddly his mother had

looked at him when he had told her *Oh, Mum, I love you sooo much*, almost as if she didn't know the word "love" or what it meant. And then with dread in his gizzard, he remembered her other words to him: "You must learn to hate, Nyroc. I shall help you learn to hate."

Gwyndor was right. He must find out the truth for himself. What he had seen in the fire was a strange and bloody history. It began with his father when he was even younger than Nyroc, pushing his brother, Soren, from the nest. And then he saw his mother trying to kill another owl who looked remarkably like Soren, possibly a sister. He had seen quick flashing images of murderous rampages. Finally, Nyroc saw the cave where his father had died, and it was not his uncle Soren trying to kill his father, but quite the reverse, his father trying to kill his uncle Soren. Then another owl had flown in. It looked like a Great Gray and in one powerful stroke with a glittering sword, he had broken his father's back. The fire had roiled with blood and murder.

He needed to get away from the Pure Ones — and especially his mother — to think about all he had seen. To find out if the flames had lied. He could not go alone, however, for the places he really needed to go to seek out the truth were the other owl kingdoms. Dustytuft was older, more experienced. Dustytuft knew the lay of the land and the way out of the canyonlands to other places. He knew how to navigate through all kinds of weather. Nyroc suddenly realized a new truth: Dustytuft's skills had been frightfully wasted by the Pure Ones, simply because he was not considered pure enough. He had been given the lowliest tasks and yet he had come here with plenty of experience — he had, after all, escaped a forest fire, navigated through the smoke and poisoned air with his da, and yet he had been treated like some ignorant, useless owl unfit for anything. Sheer stupidity on the part of the Pure Ones. Well, he would not be so stupid. He would take Dustytuft . . . *No*, Nyroc thought, *I will never call him Dustytuft again. He is Phillip. Together Phillip and I will find the truth.*

He had to tell Phillip, and they must leave right now even though the sun was over the horizon. They must risk crows. They must risk the tangled maze of the canyonlands. They must risk his mum's vengeance.

Just before he stepped onto the ledge to fly off, he looked back at his mum in the morning shadows of the stone hollow. She was a beautiful owl, the most beautiful he had ever seen, despite the scar that ran like a fine line across her face. *I am leaving*, Nyroc thought, *all that I have ever known, and all that I have ever believed in. I am leaving my rock hollow and my bedding, fluffed with the down from my mother's* own breast. I am leaving this cliff's cool shade in the summer, this cliff's ledges and overhangs and its shelter against the bite of winter's wind. I am leaving the colors that stream through the rocks that made me think of sunsets. I am leaving the fat rats that my mum is so good at catching, and the foxes that I would never dare to go after but that taste so good. I am leaving my mum, the hunter. I am leaving my mum, the murderer.

And with that last thought, Nyroc spread his wings and stepped into the air.

# CHAPTER THIRTEEN
## Negotiating with Crows

W ake up!" Nyroc shook the Sooty who slept on a stone perch on the far side of the cliff, in one of the less desirable hollows that faced the prevailing wind. Nyroc leaned in close to his friend's ear slit. "Phillip!" he whispered.

"What? What?" the Sooty Owl was immediately awake. "Oh, hi, Nyroc." He blinked again. "Nyroc, it's full morning. What are you doing here? You should be asleep back in your hollow."

"No. We have to get out, Phillip, right now. I'll explain later."

"What?"

"I told you. I can't explain now." There was no way that he could explain to Phillip right now what he had seen in the fire. He knew he had to be away, a long way away from his mum. He had to think about things, and he had to ask Phillip a lot of questions that the Sooty might not want to answer while surrounded by Pure Ones. "Just think of this as a quest, Phillip." Nyroc paused. "A quest for truth," he said solemnly. "I need your help."

Phillip blinked in astonishment. It was one thing waiting attendance on the heir of the Tytonic Union in various ceremonies. But it was quite another being asked to join him as an equal, it seemed, in a quest — a noble quest for truth. Yes, indeed, it sounded quite noble to him.

"But how will we get out of here? There are crows in the daylight."

"We have no choice," Nyroc replied.

"During the last great battle against Ga'Hoole, during The Burning, I was posted on the far side of the canyonlands. I know that territory. If we fly out of the Great Horns it will be too easy for them to follow us. Besides, there are always lookouts there. But not on the far side of the canyonlands. But, Nyroc, what is this truth you are in search of and where do you think we should go in search of it?"

Nyroc ignored the question of *what* truth and stuck to the *where* of it.

"I am not sure. Maybe The Barrens, maybe the forest kingdom of Ambala." Nyroc then took a deep breath. "Maybe the Great Ga'Hoole Tree." Nyroc amazed himself. He had actually said the words "Great Ga'Hoole Tree" out loud.

Phillip was stunned. "The great tree!" he exclaimed.

*Insane!* he thought. But he tried not to betray just how crazy he thought this notion was. He tried to sound reasonable.

"But why, Nyroc? You know all talk of the Great Ga'Hoole Tree is forbidden. You know how awful that place is."

"No, I don't know. I want to find out the truth for myself."

"For yourself," Phillip repeated in a whisper filled with awe. This sounded peculiar — and dangerous — to the Sooty Owl.

"Why not?"

"Well, first of all, the most direct route to the Island of Hoole takes you right through some terrible currents of air called the Shredders. Real hag winds. The Guardians of Ga'hoole can fly them because they are fantastic fliers. They can fly in any weather."

"Couldn't we get to the Island of Hoole some other way?" Nyroc asked.

Phillip blinked at him. *Is this owl yoicks or what? He thinks he can simply fly to the Great Ga'Hoole Tree where the Guardians live? He's the hootin' image of his mum. We are the enemy of Ga'Hoole.* But he couldn't bear to tell the young owl this. It would be hard enough for him to find a place he could live in peace *anywhere* in the owl kingdoms. He simply looked too much like Nyra and Kludd and they were feared and hated everywhere — even though Kludd was dead. There had, in fact, been rumors of his scroom. Phillip had heard Uglamore and Stryker talking about it one night. "Well, Nyroc. We'll think about that later. You might be able to find a lot of the truth you seek on the way, outside of the canyonlands."

"Yes, that is exactly what I was thinking. We must leave here for a while." *And maybe forever*, Nyroc thought.

And so they did, in broad daylight while the rest of the Pure Ones slept in their hollows. Flying almost due north, the two owls sought a warm thermal current to boost their flight. "This is an easy wind to fly," Nyroc said.

"Exactly, easy for us but difficult for any bird flying in from the opposite direction. That's why they never expected the Guardians of Ga'Hoole to come from that direction and especially over The Needles."

"What are The Needles?"

"You'll see them soon enough. That's where the Shredders begin. But remember — we're not going there, not yet, at least."

"We'll find another way to the great tree. There must be a way."

But Phillip did not reply. The less said about these yoickish plans of Nyroc, the better.

Very soon, Nyroc saw the rocky red spires scratching the sky. The two owls carved a turn to the east now and were flying parallel to a long cliff wall, when suddenly they saw what appeared to be a black cloud roll out from the wall. Nyroc blinked.

"Crows!" Phillip screamed.

Nyroc felt his wings begin to collapse. *Glaux, I'm going to yeep.* Then he remembered suddenly. Once when his mother had been very, very angry because he had done something imperfectly, she had screeched at him. She had called him "yeepish." It was the worst thing she had ever said to him. Her voice, her gizzard-searing voice, came back to him now, at this very moment. "You are a yeepish sort of owl, hatchling. Get yourself some gallgrot! Shameful yeepish little pellet, you. Pellet! Not even that. You might as well be a wet pooper." To be compared to a wet-pooping bird was one of the worst insults an owl could throw at another. *I am not yeepish!* The words exploded in Nyroc's head.

At about the same time that these four words roared through his brain and stiffened his gizzard, he heard the thuds of a rat, scurrying below. Without thinking, he plunged into a kill-spiral. Forget that this was the biggest prey he had ever gone after. It was perhaps instinct that led him to strike at the back of the rat's neck. He was hurling downward at a dizzying speed and although he probably was lighter in weight than the rat, his sharp beak delivered a fatal blow. Immediately, he scooped up the dead rodent in his talons.

"What are you doing?" Phillip was beside him now.

"Help me carry this rat. It's heavy."

Phillip slipped in beside him and grasped the rat by the tail.

"But what are we doing? The crows are gaining on us."

And then, with real shock, Phillip felt Nyroc begin to turn directly toward the crows. The blood from the rat's broken neck flew back in their faces, staining the white disk of Nyroc's disklike face. It was now the crows' turn to be shocked.

"You want this rat?" Nyroc shouted. "It's all yours." The young Barn Owl must have looked especially fearsome with his blood-splattered face. "Follow us," he called, and began flying toward a nearby rock ledge. He set the dead rat down on the ledge. The crows hovered hungrily nearby.

"What are you doing, Nyroc?" Phillip asked in a quivering voice.

"We're going to get out of this. Just listen, Phillip."

*I'm all ear slits*, the Sooty thought, and watched in amazement.

Nyroc seemed to grow bigger as he faced the crows

with a classic thronkenspeer, or threat display, his plumage ruffled and raised, swelling himself to almost twice his normal size. "This rat is a lot tastier than we are with our hollow bones and feathers. This is red meat! Enough for all of you," Nyroc yelled at the crows. He lowered his head and spread his wings, tipping them slightly forward so that the upper surfaces faced the crows. He swung his head from side to side and between his words he hissed and clacked his beak.

*This is absolutely brilliant,* thought Phillip. Crows were not very good hunters. They were just good bullies. Usually, they had to settle for the leftovers from another predator's kill. Rarely did they taste fresh meat with the blood still running out of it. Then Phillip saw Nyroc begin a gesture of the threat display that only Barn Owls make. As he began the next part of the speech, Nyroc bowed deeply — it would never be mistaken for a bow of servitude or respect — and began shaking his head rapidly as he spoke.

"This rat is yours if you give us free passage," Nyroc said.

The lead crow looked at the young Barn Owl. Nyroc was not sure what the crow was thinking. Was he imagining that next to this fat rat, he and Phillip would make a pretty miserable meal? The crows settled on a ledge across from the one where he and Phillip perched.

"The blood's still running out of this animal. It's not getting any tastier. Better make up your mind." A few more seconds passed and then the crows approached the rat.

"Not so fast!" Nyroc shreed. *Glaux*, he thought, *I sound like a full-grown owl.* Even Phillip blinked at him. "Not one bite until you send one of your mob off to tell the other crows that we get to fly free through daylight."

*Smart!* thought Phillip. *How did this young owl, barely beyond being a hatchling, figure all this out?*

Nyroc felt a tremor pass through his gizzard. *It's working! It's working!*

Yes, it worked. But crows were not the only problem for Nyroc and Phillip.

As the sun began to set, the most deadly danger of all was just starting to awaken.

# CHAPTER FOURTEEN
## The Chase Begins

Nyra had just woken up in the stone nest. She blinked several times as she looked toward the pile of down and lichen where Nyroc usually slept. "Most unusual," she murmured. "Now where could he have gone?" *Maybe out to fetch a mouse for tweener,* she thought. *That would be nice.*

Every day of Nyroc's life, Nyra had gone out for the tweener mouse or rat. *About time he started doing a little of the work around the nest.* As a matter of fact, that was one of the things she despised most about being a mum. You always had to be feeding them, doing all the work. It was definitely a two-owl job. And here she was a poor widow. She looked down at her breast, which was nearly plucked bare. What a sight she was! "Oh, Kludd," she sighed.

She went out and perched on the edge of the hollow. Stryker, one of her best lieutenants, flew by. "So tonight's the big night," he said in passing.

"Yes, yes, the Special ceremony for Nyroc. And my fine young lad I do believe went to hunt tweener for me."

"Good boy — a plummel off his old man, I'd say." But almost as soon as he said it, Stryker knew he had made a mistake.

"I would say the old lady had something to do with it!" Nyra snapped back.

"Oh, yes, Mam. Yes, Mam." Stryker had begun to loop back in his flight to apologize.

"And kindly call me General. General Mam, if you must. But General. Do remember, Stryker."

"I shall, General. General Mam."

"Excellent!" Nyra nodded, and Stryker flew off.

Blyrric, a sergeant missing one eye, alighted on a ledge between Nyra's hollow and that of her first lieutenant, Uglamore. "Anyone see Dustytuft?"

Nyra felt a slight nausea stir in her gizzard. *Dustytuft's not around? Nor Nyroc?* "You checked out the hollow where the Sooty Owls roost?" she asked.

"Yes, Mam — I mean, General Mam," Blyrric replied, for he had arrived just on the heels of the reprimand Nyra had given to Stryker.

Uglamore turned to her. "You said that Nyroc was out hunting, General?"

"I hope he is," Nyra said quietly. But the nausea was already turning to dread — and anger. She remembered how strangely Nyroc had behaved last night in their evening flight. His disturbing silences interrupted by odd questions. Had he somehow learned something he should not have found out about Tupsi? It was very important that the ceremony be shrouded in secrecy until the last minute. Had she been right about the yeepishness that she had sensed beneath his shining armor of perfection? Nyra had often heard other young owls whispering that Nyroc was too good to be true. She had attributed this to jealousy. But was he, indeed, too good to be true?

Anguish flowed through her now. Her gizzard contorted painfully. "How could he do this?" she screeched in a shree that seemed to almost split the rock off the cliffs. "Yeepish splat of a wet pooper! Though my blood flows in his veins, he deserts me like the miserable spawn of some vile spirit!" Nyra raged into the sunset that spilled on the horizon like a bloodied egg.


It did not take the owls long to organize. Stryker, the best tracker, was sent out immediately to look for pellets or any sign of them.

*If only we had one of those Ga'hoolian trackers*, Nyra thought. *Fat chance.*

Uglamore, seeming to read her mind, spoke up. "But, General, we might employ other trackers as well."

"Doc Finebeak?" she asked hopefully.

"Perhaps."

"See to it, Uglamore. If we find the hatchling, you shall be a colonel."

Nyroc and Phillip had just landed on the ragged edge of a deep-cut canyon when they first spotted the owls tracking them.

"It's a posse. I don't believe it," Phillip gasped.

"What do you mean? What's a posse?"

"Stryker always leads the posses. They track and capture. We've got to get out of here *now*!"

But both owls were exhausted. They had been flying all day and the night was just beginning.

"How did they ever find us?" Nyroc asked. And this would not be the last time he would ask this question.

"We should have buried our pellets. No more yarping midflight."

"But still!" Nyroc murmured.

"Follow me."

"Phillip, where are you going?"

"Down!"

The shadows gathered densely in the bottom of the canyon.

"Why down?"

"I'll explain later. But when we land, watch out for rattlesnakes."

"Rattlesnakes?" Nyroc had heard about rattlers. They often attacked birds who came in for a ground kill of a rodent. Seconds after a bird pounced on its prey and was delivering the death peck a rattlesnake would suddenly spring from nowhere and strike at the owl. The snake would bind itself around the owl's legs and talons, making them useless, and then hissing, plunge its fangs directly into the owl's breast to inject the poison. It was said to be a terrible death. Making a deal with crows was one thing, Nyroc thought, but rattlesnakes? No.

The two owls landed very carefully.

"Keep close to the canyon walls," Phillip whispered. "Do not yarp, and don't rustle your wings."

"What are we going to do?" Nyroc replied in a hushed voice.

"Look for an empty burrow."

Nyroc knew that there were all sorts of animals — small and not so small — that lived at the base of the canyons.

They had not been walking for long when they heard something like a sandy whisper scrape across the ground. *Fryke!* The command word for "conceal and freeze" blasted through both owls' brains. Even their gizzards seemed to lock. Nyroc had never heard the low hiss of a rattlesnake but he did not need to be told that this was it. The snake was near. The two owls' plumage grew sleek and they seemed to diminish in size as they wilfed. Both Nyroc's and Phillip's eyes closed shut until they were mere slits, but all the while one eye was held slightly open and alert for the danger. It was called "the peeping eye."

It *was* a rattlesnake. And it was slithering a few feet away from them. To fly would reveal their presence with no guarantee of escape. Staying concealed was their only hope. This was not learned behavior. It was completely instinctual. Their mottled coloring — on Nyroc, tawny browns and blacks, and, on Phillip, a sootish gray and brown — was the perfect camouflage. It helped them blend in perfectly with canyon walls.

Nyroc could hear the posse overhead, as well as the snake's progress on the ground. He knew they could not de-fryke until the sound of the snake's scraping had disappeared entirely. It seemed like hours until they could open their eyes wide and carefully begin to creep about the ground to search for a burrow or cave of some sort. They kept close to the shadowy rock wall and dared not look in the center where an almost full-shine moon flooded the canyon floor with light. Finally, after nearly an hour as the night began to turn chilly, they found a burrow.

"It's a fox's den," Phillip said as they stepped into the cavity in the rock wall. They both stood very still and adjusted their eyes to the nearly complete darkness.

"Red fox, I believe," Phillip added, noting a patch of reddish fur under his talon. "Actually, I think this was a birthing den."

"A what?" Nyroc asked.

"Foxes are odd that way. They have different dens for different things. During the breeding and birthing seasons, they usually find a separate den to live in."

"Is this birthing season?" Nyroc asked, his voice taut with anxiety.

"Luckily not. Don't worry," Phillip said. "This place is empty. I can tell."

Nyroc blinked at his friend. "You're awfully smart, Phillip. I sure am glad you're here."

"I'm just older than you are, Nyroc. There's stuff that I have seen that you haven't, and that's why I know it. But look at you. Had you ever been mobbed by crows before?"

"No," he admitted.

"Had you ever even seen a crow before?"

"No."

"So how did you know how to speak to them, to offer

them that rat, to gain us free passage through all of the light of day so that we would never be bothered by crows?"

"I don't know. I just thought real hard, I guess."

"*That* is really being smart," Phillip concluded. "Smarter than just seeing stuff and knowing it from experience as I have."

"But tell me about what you have seen, Phillip." Nyroc was still amazed that the Sooty Owl had so quickly known it was a red fox's den, and a birthing one at that. "I really want to know. All I've ever seen is the burnt-up canyonlands. I've never even seen a living, growing tree. Please tell me about the rest of the world."

Phillip blinked and thought a moment, then began to speak. "I've seen the red fox on a snowy morning, and I shall never forget the color of its fur. I've seen an eagle take down a wolf." Nyroc blinked in surprise at that. "I've seen a bear cub drown in a stream and watched her mother rage and weep and curse the very water, which quenched her thirst, for taking her cub. And I've seen a mother fox and her babies leave a den just like this. And," he hesitated. "I saw my father pick off one of those babies as the mum's back was turned. And I ate it because da and I were near to starving."

"You were, Phillip?"

"Yes, I was."

Nyroc suddenly realized that although he had known Phillip since the day he had hatched, he did not really know him at all.

"How did you come to the Pure Ones, Phillip? And why? Didn't you have a mum? You only ever speak of your da." Nyroc wanted to know everything.

"It's a long, long story, Nyroc, and I'm hungry now."

"But we can't go out. Where will we get food?"

"These birthing caves go deep and long. There are bound to be some mice around. Let's find some, and then I think you must first tell me *your* story, Nyroc."

"*My* story?" Nyroc blinked.

"What is this quest for truth, Nyroc? You promised to tell me. Why are we flying away? What kind of truth is worth risking our lives for? Your mum is chasing us with a posse!"

"Phillip," Nyroc began slowly and carefully. This would be hard to explain. "Phillip, have you ever seen pictures in the flames of a fire?"

"No. Definitely not." Phillip shook his head slowly as if trying to imagine such a thing.

"Well, I have. Gwyndor thinks that I might have something called fire sight."

"Fire sight!" Phillip said, his voice taut with awe. "Yes, I think I've heard of that. But, Nyroc — you? You have fire sight?"

"Yes. And I saw something in the fire that was horrible."

"What did you see?"

"I saw my father's death, Phillip."

"Don't say it! Don't say it." Phillip quickly stuck his head under his wings so as not to hear. "If I hear it, I shall die."

"You shall die if you hear that it was not my uncle Soren who killed my da but a huge Great Gray? I don't understand."

It was several seconds before Phillip pulled his head out from under his wing. He had wilfed to half his normal size. "Nyroc, when you hatched, word came down that we were never, ever to speak about your father's death. If anyone violated that rule, they would be killed instantly."

"Then it is true and everyone knew — everyone except me."

"Yes, the rest of us had heard the stories about what really went on in that last battle with the Guardians of Ga'Hoole."

"There was no backdraft that forced my da and his troops into the cave, was there?"

"No. Just the opposite. The Pure Ones led the Guardians into that cave. It was a trap. They were holding one of the

Guardians hostage, one of your uncle's best friends, a Burrowing Owl named Digger, I think."

"Tell me how it really happened."

"Soren and your father were engaged in a fierce fight. They were fencing back and forth. Soren held an ice sword. Your father wore fire claws. Some say that Soren hesitated at a crucial moment. It was as if he could not bring himself to kill his own brother. But then there was this silvery blur in the cave. It was the Great Gray. . . ."

Phillip continued with the story. It was exactly what Nyroc had seen in the flames. When the Sooty Owl had finished speaking, there was a thick silence in the fox's den. Finally, Nyroc spoke. "I saw other horrible things in the fire, as well. I saw my mother on a killing rampage. She was smeared with blood — and not just from battles. She seemed to be killing lone owls for no reason at all. I saw her trying to kill a very young female Barn Owl who looked a lot like Soren."

"That would be Eglantine, his sister."

"I have an aunt, then? My mum tried to kill her, as well?"

"There are rumors. We sometimes hear things from Rogue smiths — and others. Forbidden things. I don't know if it is true. Some say Eglantine smashed the egg that Nyra had laid before yours. Remember, Nyroc, I was young when I first came to the Pure Ones. Some of these things that you saw in the flames might have happened when I was too young to understand, or even before I came to the Pure Ones with my da. There were always rumors."

"What were the rumors about Ga'Hoole? Tell me about Ga'Hoole."

Phillip shut his eyes for a long time. "I can't believe I am telling you all this." He opened his eyes finally and blinked rapidly. "You know, if I tell you all this I shall never be able to return to them."

"Do you want to return?"

"Good question." Phillip sighed. "Do you?"

"Not until I know the complete truth."

"I can only tell you what I've heard. What I cannot tell you is if it is rumor or truth."

"Go ahead."

"The Great Ga'Hoole Tree is a special place and so are the legends surrounding it. I think that is why Nyra forbade all talk of it. It seems that at the great tree, owls really do think for themselves. They decide things themselves, or so it is rumored. They learn not only how to read and write, but they learn many mysteries."

"What kind of mysteries?"

"Mysteries of science and of stars, how the stars move in the sky, of air and weather currents, of fire and ice. They

not only make weapons from iron but other things —
complicated things. And it is said that there are all kinds of
owls living together there. Barn Owls are not considered
the finest or the best. There are high-ranking Spotted
Owls and Snowies and Burrowing Owls, even important
Pygmy and Elf Owls."

"Pygmy and Elf!" Nyroc was astounded.

"It is said that there are few rules. Nothing is really forbidden."

"Nothing spronk?"

"Absolutely not. As a matter of fact, there was once a
rumor that an elderly Burrowing Owl had declared a book
from their library spronk, and she was disciplined for it."

Nyroc's beak dropped open. He was speechless.

"But, as I said," Phillip continued, "I don't know what
is rumor and what is truth. For us, however, it was completely forbidden to talk of the great tree except to say the
very worst things imaginable."

"Like when I was told that they eat owl eggs to give
them courage?"

"Yes. I never believed that one," Phillip scoffed.

"I don't know what to believe," Nyroc said miserably.
"Maybe I'm just seeing things in the fire that don't exist at
all. Maybe what you've heard about what my mother and
father did is not true." He looked up anxiously at Phillip.

"I can't answer that for you, Nyroc."

Nyroc sighed. "All right, now tell me your story. You promised."

Phillip had always felt that his own story was a sad one. But he now realized that Nyroc's story might be even sadder as he quested for the truth about his parents.

# CHAPTER FIFTEEN
## Phillip's Story

W e came from Silverveil, one of the most beautiful
forests in the entire owl universe."

"Full of trees with green leaves?" Nyroc asked.

"Yes, and green needles, too, like spruce and fir and
pine. You've never seen so many trees in all your life."

"I've never seen *any* trees in all my life," Nyroc replied.

"I suppose not. Well, Silverveil is one of the most beautiful forests. But there was the occasional forest fire."

"That's awful," Nyroc said, thinking of his experience
of living in the barren, burnt-out canyonlands.

"You'd think so. But fires can help a forest to grow. They
clear out old dead trees. With pine trees, it takes years for
their cones to open up and release seeds for new trees. But
when there's a fire, the cones pop and the seeds spread."

"Don't the seeds burn?"

"No. It's like a miracle. Out of the destruction comes
new life." Phillip paused and then whispered to himself,
"For some."

Nyroc tipped his head and blinked. "For some, Phillip?"

"For my family, it was the end. It was in a forest fire that I lost my mum, my sisters and brothers, and, really, my father."

"But you said you came here with your father."

"He might as well have been lost," Phillip answered bitterly.

"I don't understand."

Phillip sighed deeply. "My mum and da were quite different from each other. My mum, you see, had aspirations."

"What are aspirations?" Nyroc asked.

"Hopes, dreams. She came from a very old family of Silverveil, one of the oldest, a noble family from the time that Silverveil had kings and queens. If they had still had them she would have been a princess. Sometimes my da even called her princess. She liked that." Phillip's eyes softened as if he were dreaming of something long ago.

"But my da was different. He was a meat-and-insect kind of fellow. You fly out. You get the vole, the mouse, the occasional small fox — very occasional. My father was not happy when he had to pick off that baby fox. I mean, Da, he had his standards. Oh, that he did!"

"What do you mean by standards?" Nyroc asked.

"Oh, you know, rules — rules you make up for yourself, not the ones that others give you. When you decide for yourself what's right and wrong."

Nyroc was intrigued. "What do these standards do?"

"Do?" Phillip was puzzled. How could he explain this? It wasn't as if these standards were practical. They didn't "do" much in the practical sense. "They aren't rules like the Pure Ones have — like you can't carry a certain kind of weapon if you're not of a certain rank or like all the rules against us Sooties. These kinds of rules, standards, well, they just make you a better owl." That, Phillip suddenly realized, had been the tragedy of his father. He had been a better owl at one time, a really fine owl. Before he joined the Pure Ones.

"Oh," Nyroc said quietly. "But what happened when the forest fire came? You said you lost your father. But he didn't die then."

"I'll try to explain. The fire broke out in the daytime. It was so fierce that it jumped the Silver River. The smoke was terribly thick. It was impossible to see. Smoke stung our eyes and filled our throats so we could hardly breathe. We were all together fleeing our hollow in a part of Silverveil called The Brooklets.

"Somehow my da and I got separated from Mum and my brothers and sisters. I begged my father to go back and look for them. He said no. It would be useless. He was probably right. But soon enough, I could tell that he regretted that he had not gone back. After the fire burned itself out, there was nothing left of The Brooklets. We went back. But we found no sign of Mum or the rest of the kids. We looked everywhere, flying from one part of the forest to another.

"I could tell that my father regretted more and more each day that he had not even tried to rescue them. He stopped hunting for a while and just moped about. Worst case of the gollymopes I'd ever seen. I was really hungry. You have to understand, I was younger than you are now. I had no hunting skills.

"But it was something worse than just the gollymopes with Da. He had this terrible anger. He would strike out at me for no reason. There was something wrong with his gizzard, with his mind.

"The worst of winter was soon upon us. We were starving. Game was scarce. It was at this time that we found the fox's den and Da went after the baby. Da had always said that it was wrong to kill the young of any prey because if you did that, they would not grow up to have children of their own and then there would be no animals left to hunt. So I knew how Da had broken his own rule here. But we were starving. It wasn't long after the killing of the baby fox that I noticed other changes in Da, small ones at first. It was as if he didn't care about anything. He cursed in front of me, which he had never ever done before."

*Never?* Nyroc thought. Nyroc recalled how his mum cursed in front of him all the time.

Phillip continued, "It was also around this same time that Wortmore showed up with Stryker. This is one of the Pure Ones' best strategies for finding new recruits. They go into regions where forest fires have destroyed the land, where owls feel lost, confused, disoriented, and are almost starving to death. They promise them a good hollow with soft moss, plump voles, and rock rats. The new recruits are promised a chance to become the pioneers and leaders of a new empire."

"But the Pure Ones only recruit Barn Owls, right?"

"Yes. Stryker and Wortmore said that only Barn Owls were worthy of joining this elite union. That the Union must be kept pure and only Barn Owls were pure enough."

"I know that's what Mum always tells me — that we Barn Owls are Glaux's favorites."

"Yes, but what they didn't tell us was that some Barn Owls are *more pure* than others. No, no. My da thought he was going to be a big important squadron leader. He had become very bitter. It seemed that now that he had lost most of his family, he was ready to kill."

"So what happened when your father joined?"

"What happened? Ha! He got killed!"

"Killed?"

"In the first battle he ever went into. Kludd had managed to kidnap one of the leaders of the Ga'Hoole Tree. But the great tree sent the Chaw of Chaws to rescue him."

"I know of the Chaw of Chaws. I heard Mum talk about it. I think my uncle Soren was a leader of it. Was he the one who killed your father?"

"No, it was a Short-eared Owl. Female. I forget her name. She is supposed to be an incredible flier — fast, with unbelievable precision."

"Not the Great Gray who killed my father, then."

"No, not Twilight."

"Twilight? Is that what they call him?"

"Yes."

Nyroc now knew the name of his father's killer.

A silence stretched between the two friends. Outside the den, they could hear the wind whipping through the narrow canyon. An occasional gust of snow was sucked into the den from a downdraft. Finally, Nyroc spoke. "So what happened to you after your da died?"

"Nothing good. Without him, I was just another mouth to feed. Because I was a Sooty, I was given the most menial tasks and never trained for the elite units. I was miserable until you came along. Then everything changed." Phillip shook his head in wonder. "I was the one chosen to be the closest friend, companion to the hatchling, the little chick that had emerged from the egg they called the Sacred Orb. My life changed. I got the choice pieces of freshly killed vole. I got to fly out and gather insects for your First Insect ceremony. I occupied a place of honor at all your First Ceremonies — right next to your mum. And although I did not much care for Nyra, I was liking, loving you more every day."

Again there was silence. Nyroc peeked out of the den. "It's really dark out there now."

"Yes," Phillip replied, "but I think it would be foolish to leave. We should stay here until daylight. Less chance of them keeping up the chase through the daylight. Besides" — Phillip gave a wink to Nyroc — "they don't have a free pass from the crows."

"That's right. I never thought of that."

"So let's rest up and wait for daybreak."

So the two friends wedged themselves into the most comfortable corner they could find and tried to fall asleep. But Nyroc couldn't sleep. Too many thoughts were swirling through his head. His gizzard was in a twitter.

"Phillip, you still awake?"

"Sort of," Phillip replied sleepily.

"I was wondering.... Was your name really Phillip when you were a young owlet and lived back there in Silverveil?"

"I can't exactly remember. It began with a *P-h*, I'm pretty sure."

"What's a *P-h*?" Nyroc said.

"It's a letter or two letters."

"A letter?"

"Yeah, for reading and writing. My mum knew how to read. She taught me my letters."

"You mean that it's not just the Guardians of Ga'Hoole who know how to read and write?"

"They know better than any other owls, but no, they are not the only ones. Some owls do learn a bit about letters."

"Can you read?"

"A little bit."

"I'd like to learn how to read," Nyroc replied. There was a wistfulness in his voice.

"I can teach you the letters of your name, but to really learn, you'd have to go to the Great Ga'Hoole Tree."

"Phillip . . ." Nyroc began.

"I'm really tired, Nyroc. We should get some sleep."

"I promise this is the last question."

"All right. What?"

"Well, isn't it odd that both our fathers were killed by the Guardians of Ga'Hoole, and that we've both lost our mothers?"

At this, Phillip's eyes blinked wide open. "Nyroc, I lost my mother. Your mother lost you. There's a difference."

"You mean I left."

"Yes, and with good reason."

"What do you mean good reason?"

"To seek the truth and . . ." Phillip hesitated.

"And what?"

"Nyroc, you were too fine for her, too very fine. You have standards, Nyroc. Standards!"

*Standards*, Nyroc thought.

*But standards aren't practical*, Phillip thought. *You can't eat standards. You can't live in them.*

Finally, the young owls fell asleep.

# CHAPTER SIXTEEN

# A Speck in the Sky

A thin ribbon of light lay diagonally across Phillip's facial disk. He blinked one eye open. *Morning,* he thought miserably. Owls were supposed to go to sleep in the morning and rise at night. "Everything's turned frinking upside down," he muttered to himself. Nyroc was still sleeping peacefully in his corner. No sense waking him up until he had a peek outside. He walked over to the opening of the den and poked his head out. "Ooph!" he exclaimed, clamping his eyes shut. The sunlight splintered blindingly across a thin blanket of white snow. He dared to open his eyes in a half squint and look up to see if there was any sign of the posse. He searched the sky for several minutes, flipping his head this way and that. It was a beautiful day — if one was a day kind of creature. Very little wind. The sky was a brilliant flawless blue and there was no sign whatsoever of the posse. Time to wake up Nyroc. Except for the unfortunate fact that it was daylight, the conditions were perfect for flying.

"Nyroc! Nyroc! Time to go." He gave his friend a shake. "Come on, we have to make time while we can in the day. I don't think they will be flying."

Then as the two birds made their way to the edge of the den, Phillip suddenly remembered something. "Hold it!" He slammed Nyroc back with one wing just before he had stepped into the fresh snow.

"What's the matter?"

"We can't take off from out there. We'll leave talon prints in the snow. Stryker will find them. We'll have to do a dry takeoff."

"I've never done one," Nyroc said.

"Don't worry. They're easy. We'll practice in here."

"In here?" Nyroc looked around the confines of the den.

A dry takeoff was one from the ground when there was no perch — branch, rock, or limb — available, and very little room to spread one's wings in the normal way.

"All right, Nyroc, now watch me." With a great *whoosh*, Phillip lifted his wings straight up into a sharp V shape. Then he slashed downward in a power stroke. Instantly, he was aloft. He flew out of the den and then back in. "Now you try it."

It took Nyroc just a few times before he mastered it.

"Now here's the next thing," Phillip said.

"Next? What do you mean? I did it perfectly that time. Let's just go."

"Look down. There are talon marks all over the floor of this den. If Stryker came in here he would find them. See that pile of lichen over there? You take part of it and I'll take part and we'll sweep the marks away."

It did not take them long to erase the signs of their presence in the fox's den. Nyroc's dry takeoff was flawless, and together the birds rose higher and higher out of the canyon.

It was a lovely day for flying, even for dedicated night fliers. There was the extra shimmer of excitement as they flew past a cliff line with crows and saw twenty or more of them nod their heads in a silent salute.

"How about that!" Phillip shouted, and slid in next to Nyroc. "Slam four!" and the two birds touched their four talons from their adjacent legs midflight.

They had been flying for some time when the clouds began to roll in behind them, smudging the perfect blueness of the sky. But ahead it was still clear. They were holding a north-northeast course so as to avoid the Shredders of the Shadow Forest. It was a course toward Silverveil but first they would have to cut through The Barrens. Nyroc had wanted desperately to go to Silverveil.

If he was going to see trees for the first time in his life, he wanted to see the most beautiful trees of all and that was where they grew. Phillip wanted to return because he wanted to see how much had grown back in The Brooklets since the fire.

They kept a keen lookout in case Nyra and her troops had followed them into the daylight, but so far they had seen nothing. They stopped to hunt a couple of times. They were very careful not to leave tracks of any kind — either pellets or talon marks. Nyroc now swiveled his head back toward the clouds that rolled in thicker and thicker behind him. Weather coming in — snow or rain, he guessed, this time of year. He noticed something dark in the cloud but it was just a speck. But as soon as he swiveled his head back to face forward he felt a funny little *ping* in his gizzard. This time, he flipped his head all the way back and cranked the muscles in his facial disk to orient his ear slits toward any sound that might come from that speck of darkness. He heard a rhythmic *wuff wuff wuff* . . . so soft, no other creature except a Barn Owl could have ever detected it.

"Phillip! We're being followed!"

"No!" Phillip flipped his head back and then gasped. "You're right. What should we do?"

"Split up for now," Nyroc said, surprised at the certainty

in his own voice. "It'll be harder for them to follow both of us."

"But where should we meet? I sort of know this territory, but you don't know it at all."

Nyroc thought a moment, then said, "We'll circle back. They won't expect us to do that. We'll meet back at the fox's den tonight."

Phillip had to admit it was a good idea. The overhanging ledges of the canyon gave them some protection from being seen. No owl would expect another owl to dive into a deep box canyon that was full of rattlesnakes.

"All right, let's go."

And so the two young owls peeled away from each other in opposite directions.

# CHAPTER SEVENTEEN

## Pieces of Me!

Nyroc peeked out of the fox's den to scan the sky for a sign of Phillip. He had arrived a good time before and had expected Phillip by now. But there was not a speck in the sky. Well, he supposed he should consider this lucky. There was no sign of Phillip — then again, no sign of the posse. But what if the posse had caught Phillip? That was a scary thought. Nyroc turned to walk deeper into the shadows of the den. He yarped a pellet, picked it up, and walked farther into the den to scratch out a place to bury it.

As he was digging with his talons, he felt something odd drop from his tail. He wheeled around and saw a feather, one of his undertail coverts, lying on the ground. "Great Glaux! What's happening to me?" He stared in a mixture of dismay and horror. Another smaller covert slipped lazily to the ground. He began to tremble uncontrollably and moan. His gizzard shuddered and grew squishy.

"What in Glaux's name is going on in here?" Phillip said as he flew into the den.

"Phillip! I'm so glad you're here."

"What is wrong?"

Nyroc straightened up and tried to look brave. He gulped and then blinked several times. "Phillip, I hate to tell you this but . . . but I think I am dying."

"Dying? What are you talking about? You look perfectly healthy to me."

Nyroc nodded toward his feet and then bent down and picked up one of the feathers. "How do you explain this, Phillip?"

"Explain it? What's to explain? You're molting, that's all."

"Molting?"

Phillip sighed deeply. "Hasn't that idiot mother of yours told you about molting?"

"No."

"First of all, it's natural."

"You mean I'm not ill? I'm not going to die?"

"Not from molting. Sorry to disappoint you. Molting is a sign of maturity. When you were a very young hatchling, your first fluffy down fell off and you were pretty unsightly. We had a First Molting ceremony, don't you remember?"

"Maybe I kind of remember. But what's this?" Nyroc

waved the feather in front of Phillip. "This isn't down. This is an important flight feather. An undertail covert. Lose too many of those and how will I rudder, or make a decent turn?"

"When feathers get old and worn you shed them. Another feather will be coming in a short time."

"When?"

"Don't be so impatient, Nyroc."

"I wouldn't be if I weren't being chased by my own mum, her best tracker, and her fiercest lieutenants. I need all the feathers I have."

"It'll be a few days." Phillip paused and a worried shadow fell across his eyes.

"What is it?" Nyroc was quick to detect even the subtlest emotions in his friend.

"We're going to have to bury these feathers like we buried the pellets. We don't want them able to track us through your feathers."

"Oh, Glaux! I never thought of that." Nyroc began trembling all over again.

"Let me check you to see if any others are missing."

Phillip crowded close to Nyroc and with the special edge on his middle talon began combing through the feathers. He had been Nyroc's chief preener since the young owl had hatched. Preening was one of the most pleasant social interactions an owl could have. As he picked through the feathers, he was careful to examine for any ruptured shafts where feathers might have broken away. He could feel Nyroc begin to shake once again with fear. "Find anything?" Nyroc asked desperately.

"Pull yourself together, for Glaux's sake. No, I haven't found anything."

"'Pull yourself together,' you say. Easy for you! You're not falling apart. Pieces of me could be strewn all over the canyonlands — like flares guiding them to us."

"If there was ever a time not to fall apart it is now, Nyroc," Phillip shreed at him. "You dragged me out here to find the truth about the Pure Ones and Ga'Hoole. And to do that we must escape from the Pure Ones. You are more than just your feathers. It was not feathers that spoke to those crows. It was not feathers that figured out how to bargain with them and get a free passage. You are brains and you are gizzard. Oh, yes. You made a fine thronken display with your wings, but that was nothing compared to the gallgrot in your gizzard. So don't let me hear you going on about falling apart."

Nyroc nodded. He was so ashamed. Phillip was right. If molting was a natural thing, why should he fear it? He and Phillip simply had to get out of the canyonlands. He had to survive. He wanted the truth and more — he wanted to see a tree, to know the color green, and to maybe even meet his uncle Soren someday. Indeed, the more he thought about his uncle, the more intrigued he became. And when he reflected on what had been revealed to him in the flames of Gwyndor's fires, his uncle Soren seemed a most extraordinary owl and he longed to know him.

They had just settled in to eat a vole that they had discovered deep in the den. Nyroc had pounced on it and was about to bite off its head.

"Let it go!" Phillip suddenly blurted out.

"Let it go? Are you yoicks?" Nyroc had the fat little fellow gripped in his talons.

"Let it go! They're back. We don't want a vole's blood to give us away."

Nyroc immediately dropped the vole, which scampered away. He crept up next to Phillip and peered out the small opening of the den.

"Great Glaux, they're lighting down on the canyon floor! How did they ever find us?"

"I don't know," Phillip replied grimly.

"We're trapped."

"Maybe not."

"What do you mean?"

"Remember, Nyroc, I told you that these dens are deep. Sometimes there's a back way out. Let's go!" Phillip led the way. He flipped his head back as they hopped around the first bend in the den. "If you drop any feathers, pick them up."

They walked for a very long time in very close quarters. Nyroc had taken the lead. They both felt it was better that Phillip follow in case the young owl molted a feather or two along the way. Phillip had taken some old nesting material from the fox's birthing bed and was dragging it behind him to cover their tracks. He knew Stryker was a decent tracker. But was he good enough to find them in a fox's den in a box canyon after they had split up and been so careful circling back?

"Hey, it's getting wider," Nyroc called back. "I can almost spread my wings."

"That's good." Phillip was sick of dragging this brushy stuff behind him. The passageway was damp and smelled of dead animals and the scat of creatures he didn't even want to think about. The walls seemed to weep with water, and there was no moving air. It was not a bird kind of a place at all.

"I'm flying!" Nyroc called back a few seconds later.

The two birds flew through a twisting passageway barely wider than the span of their wings. It felt as if they were flying in an upward spiral within the canyon walls. They heard rats scurrying about and occasionally the darkness was slashed by the glowing red slits of their eyes. The owls were not tempted to hunt them, even though their stomachs were empty. Indeed, all they thought of was the task. They had become the task, and the task was to escape.

"I see some light ahead," Nyroc called back.

It couldn't be much, Phillip thought, for it was almost night. And then as if to answer him, Nyroc called out, "It's a star."

They both blasted out from the close, damp, fetid air of the den into the velvety blackness of the night.

"It's Nevermoves," Phillip said. "The star that never moves. We must be flying north if we are heading toward that star."

"Aren't the Shredders to the north?" Nyroc asked.

"Yes, but don't worry. We'll change course before we get there. We'll cut into The Barrens. Lots of Burrowing Owls there, plenty of ground holes for cover."

"Dens again!" muttered Nyroc. But he knew he shouldn't complain. He quickly looked back to see if he was trailing any feathers. "Oh, Glaux! It's the posse! They're coming!" Nyroc shreed.

"How did they find us?" Phillip said. "All right. Spiral down," Phillip yelled.

"Down there?" Nyroc gasped in amazement. Below them were The Needles, sharp and stabbing at the sky. Were they even flyable? They looked so tightly packed together it was hard to imagine any space between them to light down. They were not, however, going to light down.

"This is going to be the fanciest flying you've ever done," Phillip said.

The Needles were meant to be flown over, not between, but that was exactly what the two owls were doing in hopes of confounding and losing the owls who were chasing them. Phillip and Nyroc made quick wing shifts, minute adjustments of flight feathers as they threaded their way at top speed between the rocky spires.

It would be easy to get lost within The Needles' tangled maze of stone and easy to clip all the plummels off the leading edge of one's primaries. Nyroc's muscles began to ache fiercely. He noticed that Phillip had fallen behind him for the first time. Nyroc felt every feather shaft as he had never felt them before. The tiny adjustments he had to make to his primaries, to his greater wing coverts, to his tail coverts were difficult and exhausting. But he must keep flying. *Glaux, even my talons hurt!*

What was that ahead? Nyroc blinked. There was something projecting from The Needles directly in front of him. Glaux bless, it was a sliver of rock. He settled down upon it. A moment later, Phillip joined him.

"I don't think I could have kept going," Phillip said.

"Do you think we've lost them?" Nyroc gasped.

"I don't know. Maybe. Press in as close as you can. The moon is almost full shine and we could cast shadows."

"Look, it's starting to snow again." Nyroc nodded toward some great roiling gusts of snow.

"Yeah. The Shredders are just where you see those gusts. They toss the snow into whirlpools."

Nyroc saw. It was frightening. He had never seen wind like this. It not only disturbed the snow, but the very blackness of the sky and the light of the moon looked to Nyroc as if they were swirling violently.

Phillip was looking up. He spoke quietly. "They've found us!"

Nyroc felt his gizzard drop to his talons. "No."

"Yes, but they can't figure out how to get at us."

"How long will we be safe here?"

"Not long."

"Why not?"

"Because there is only one tracker in the entire owl

126

universe who can find his way in here. Doc Finebeak."
Phillip paused. "And he's flying with them."

Nyroc looked up and saw an immense Snowy Owl
circling overhead, and between his two wings in the middle of his back another feather rose, long and black.

"What's that sticking out of his back?" Nyroc asked.

"It's a crow's feather. That's how you know it's him. The
crows love him. He's a hero to them. And he's feared."

"In other words, he has free passage," Nyroc said.

"Yes, and not just here. Everywhere." Phillip was silent
for a moment. "He'll find a way to us. Probably before that
cloud crosses the moon."

"What'll we do?"

"Not much choice, eh? Stuck between The Needles
and the Shredders."

The two owls looked at each other.

Then they both roared a great shree, "The Shredders!"
And they blasted straight up from the sliver of rock, out
and over The Needles, and headed directly toward the lac-
erating winds of the Shredders.

# CHAPTER EIGHTEEN

# Shredded

Nyra watched the Great Snowy closely as he began to speak. The Pure Ones had retreated from The Needles as soon as they saw where Nyroc and Dustytuft were heading. "We have a situation here that is most unusual." Doc Finebeak blinked and looked in the direction of the Shredders. "Only the Guardians of Ga'Hoole know how to negotiate those winds. I have never seen birds of any species, not even eagles, voluntarily hurl themselves into the Shredders. If they survive it, which I sincerely doubt, they will emerge dazed and confused."

"But how do we know for sure whether they get killed or not?" Nyra snapped.

Doc Finebeak looked at her in amazement. One of these birds was her son. She betrayed not a hint of sorrow or fear. She just wanted to be sure of his death. It seemed odd.

"I do not understand my son's rebellious ways, but I will *not* tolerate rebellion," Nyra said, as if that explained her lack of feeling.

"I see." Doc Finebeak nodded. Actually, he didn't see, but that was immaterial. Doc Finebeak came from Beyond the Beyond. Most hireclaws and owls who would do anything for some kind of payment came from there. Mercenaries seldom questioned motives or reasons as long as they got paid. Payment could be anything from hunting rights in certain closely guarded owl territories where prey was plentiful to coals from Rogue smiths, and in the old days — flecks. In their present condition, the Pure Ones did not have much to offer a superb tracker like Doc. But the Great Snowy felt that it was wise to keep in the good graces of a once-powerful force. He knew that Nyra was a formidable leader. She could rise to power again. He wanted her in his debt.

"How do we make sure?" Nyra repeated.

"There is a way around the Shredders. I am one of the few who know about it." He looked directly at Nyra and puffed out his breast a bit. He wanted Nyra to know just how valuable he was. "We will go to the spill-out points on the other side. I know those as well. That is where we will find them, if indeed they survive."

Uglamore now stepped forward. "Just how many spill-out points are there, Doc?"

"Two or three, at the most. It would be easy for me to find the one they come out of, and remember, they will be confused. Capture should be easy."

*Too easy*, Uglamore thought. This was not the first time he had had doubts about the Pure Ones, their goals, their strategies. Even before The Burning, he had wondered if there might be a better way to train soldiers. He began having these thoughts after a small battle in The Beaks. At that point, the Pure Ones had been better armed than any other group of owls. Their discipline was superb. They had conquered more territory than any other owl army except those of the Northern Kingdoms. And yet they were defeated in The Beaks by far fewer owls, owls who were reported to have little military discipline. It was then that Uglamore began to wonder if a free society like Ga'Hoole might produce a more superior soldier than the regimented one of the Pure Ones. Wits had won that skirmish, not might or discipline.

Since Nyroc's birth, he had reflected further on these notions. He was drawn to the young hatchling. He shuddered when he saw Nyra's expectations for him and how she treated him. He wondered how this young hatchling might develop if he had been hatched to a normal owl family, or even more intriguing, if he had been hatched in the Great Ga'Hoole Tree. More disturbing to Uglamore, however, were his thoughts about himself. Even though he was on the brink of achieving the rank of colonel, he had begun to grow very weary of Nyra and her ways.

But where else could an owl of his age go — especially an owl who had distinguished himself for fighting with the most hated union of owls in the world? It was not the defeat at the Battle of The Burning itself that had depressed him but the thought of a future living with the Tytonic Union of Pure Ones. That was when he began to think about the egg that held the new life that would be Nyroc. He actually began to dread the hatching out. And on the night of the eclipse when the egg did hatch out, he had experienced a deep feeling in his gizzard that he could only have described as sorrowful joy. It was said that owls born on such a night as this had upon them an enchantment that gave them unusual powers. Uglamore knew this little hatchling would have powers, but what would they bring him?

So capture would be easy, Doc had said. But perhaps death in the Shredders would be easier for Nyroc. If he did survive, what did he face with his mum? He would be made to go through with the Special ceremony, which he himself had never questioned until now.

*Yes*, thought Uglamore, *I passed my Special by killing my dear cousin. So enchanted was I with the old High Tyto, Kludd's predecessor, that I very soon got over his death.* He had rationalized it to himself until he was certain he'd done the right thing. At the time, it hadn't seemed to matter nearly as much as his own ascendancy in the inspiring collection of Barn Owls that would one day rule the world. He had been young then, strong, a skillful fighter, and he was most of all pure, a pure Tyto alba, not one of the lesser breeds like a Masked or a Sooty. Now he wasn't so sure. Now he had questions.

"Does that answer your question about the spillways, Uglamore?" Nyra asked crisply.

He was about to say *No, General Mam, it does not.* But he was not a young owl anymore. He was beyond his middle years and he had nowhere to go. He would be cast out of any civilized group of owls. So instead he replied, "Yes, General Mam, that certainly does."

"We will follow Doc Finebeak to the other side of the Shredders to see if Nyroc is . . ." It was seldom that Nyra hesitated in speaking. She began again. "To see what the outcome is."

*Outcome,* thought Uglamore. *She means, will she find her son dead? And if he is alive, what then?* Uglamore had not meant for this question to pop out. But it did. "General Mam, if Nyroc is alive, what shall be done then?"

"He is a rebellious owl. He shall be disciplined. If he had exhibited this behavior in battle it would be considered treason and he would have to face the most dire consequences. But he is young and he is rebellious. And I shall give him a second chance."

*Some chance*, thought Uglamore.

Nyroc had managed to keep Phillip in his sight for a few seconds after entering the Shredders. But as he was tossed and spun by the wild winds, it felt as if both parts of his stomach had crashed into each other. He did not know which way was up or down. He was pitched and tumbled by the cutting winds of the torrent. He thought he saw several of his tail feathers whiz by him. Would there be any feathers left? Did he care? Did he care if he lived or died?

Nyroc suddenly realized that he was tired, so very tired. Not just of being chased, but of living with his strange and frightening mother. If life as a Pure One was the only choice, would it be a relief to die in this shredding wind? That was Nyroc's last thought in the Shredders. He dimly realized he had ceased to flap his wings and he gave himself up to the lashing currents of the hag winds. The roar of the Shredders grew fainter and fainter in his ear slits.

# CHAPTER NINETEEN

## It Hurts

When Phillip tumbled out of the Shredders and was immediately captured he knew his own quest for truth had ended. The horrific meaning of the special treatment he had been granted since Nyroc's hatching began to sizzle and pop in the Sooty's gizzard like a sap tree bursting into flames: Who had been among the first owls to be brought in when the Sacred Orb, as Nyra had referred to her egg, hatched? Himself. Who had been appointed chief preener? Nyra, who had always regarded him with utter contempt, made *him* the companion for her dear hatchling. It all began to make a terrible, dreadful sense. He knew now that he had been set up as Nyroc's best friend so that he might help Nyroc prove himself worthy to become an officer in the most elite unit of the Pure Ones.

*What happened?* Nyroc wondered as he dragged himself to his feet. Every one of his hollow bones ached. He staggered forward. Then tried to spread his wings. They felt strange. "Where am I?" he wondered aloud.

"With your mother!"

He wheeled around suddenly. He could hardly believe it. How had she gotten here? Nyra looked at him sharply, coldly. "We thought you'd never come to. But you have. And except for the loss of feathers, you look quite fit." She paused. "Fit enough to kill," she added.

"What?"

"Don't pretend you don't know what I'm talking about. It is time for your Special ceremony, my dear. Be pleased I am willing to forgive your offensive behavior." Nyroc was so stunned he could hardly speak.

"Well, what do you say?" Nyra hissed at him. "Aren't you going to thank me for my generosity?"

Nyroc stared at his mother. Flames seemed to leap before his eyes. Terrible images seared his brain, sizzled in his gizzard. He simply had to know.

"Well?" Nyra asked again.

"Mum, could I speak to you alone before the Special ceremony? I need to know certain things."

She regarded him silently for a long moment before speaking. "Of course, dear." His mother flew a short distance away from the other Pure Ones who had accompanied her. Flight was too painful for Nyroc since so many of his feathers had been broken off. He waddled in a most humiliating fashion after her.

When he reached her, she was running her beak through her own sparse breast feathers. This gesture of hers always made Nyroc's gizzard squirm with guilt. "I'm quite a sight, aren't I?" She laughed softly. It seemed to break the tension.

"I missed you, Nyroc. You are all I have."

"But, Mum."

"You are my world."

*Her world? What does that mean?* Nyroc wondered. *To be her world. Is that love?*

"You are the Union, the Empire."

"But do you love *me*?" Nyroc asked.

In that moment, Nyra wilfed. Confusion and anger swam in her dark eyes. The scar that ran down her face seemed to twitch. She tried to say the word "love." Her beak opened and a guttural sound tore from it, but Nyroc did not understand it. She ran her beak through her breast feathers again. And once more, Nyroc felt that twinge of guilt in his gizzard.

"You do! I know you do, Mum."

"You shall be great, Nyroc. You shall rule not like a general but like a king, an emperor. It is your destiny. You were hatched on the night of the eclipse. Not since the ancient King Hoole has there been such an owl as you. I know it. I feel it in my gizzard."

"King Hoole," Nyroc repeated.

"Yes, King Hoole," she whispered the words. "Are you ready for the Special ceremony, my . . . my . . . my love?"

*She said it. She loves me!* "Yes, Mum. Yes. I am ready." And the images he had seen in the flames receded, then simply melted away completely. *After all,* Nyroc told himself, *she lied to me about my father's death because she wanted me to be strong — and to love him more. Yes, that must be it.*

They returned to the circle of trees where Stryker, Uglamore, and several of the other top lieutenants perched, waiting. Nyroc was so excited by his mother's proclamation of love that he did not notice at first that he was standing amid trees — real trees — just as his mother had promised. He looked at them now. "Mum, these are trees, aren't they?"

"Didn't I promise you that I would show you a living tree?"

"Oh, yes, General Mam." And Nyroc raised his talon in a perfect hail Kludd salute.

His mother's gizzard trembled with pride. "Bring forth the prisoner," she commanded. Blyrric and another officer walked in with a Sooty Owl tethered between them by vines. They quickly tied him to a tree.

Nyroc stopped in his tracks and blinked. "Phillip?"

"Who in hagsmire is Phillip?" Nyra replied.

"Go, Nyroc! Fly away!" Phillip screamed.

Nyroc peered forward and blinked. The world was coming into focus — sharply, all too sharply.

"Oh, Dustytuft. So that's what you call him. Well, you're going to call him 'dead' soon," Nyra said.

Nyroc turned toward his mother in disbelief. "But it was supposed to be an animal like a fox or . . . or . . ." Nyroc did not want to let the vile words out of his beak. Only now did the true horror of what had been planned for his Special ceremony explode in his brain. He let the words come. ". . . Or Smutty, the prisoner." He hated himself in the very core of his gizzard for saying those words. He would not do it. This was not combat. It was murder. But he had let the words tumble from his beak to keep from thinking something even more horrible.

"But that's too easy. You hardly know Smutty. Remember, I told you that the first lesson of hate is easy. You were told to hate your father's killer, Soren. Easy, right? But the second lesson would be harder."

Then the flames suddenly raged in Nyroc's brain. He felt his gizzard stir. "But Soren didn't kill my father," he blurted out. "It was the Great Gray. You told me lies. It was all lies."

"Who told him? Who told him?" Nyra screeched and flew at her lieutenants.

"Nobody told me. I saw it in the flames," Nyroc howled. "And I shall not kill Smutty — or Phillip, Mum. I shall not!"

"You must," she shreed. "You must prove yourself worthy of this Union. This Empire! You must kill someone close to you."

Another image filled Nyroc's mind. He saw a hollow in a distant fir tree. He saw two young chicks, one not even ready to fly yet. He saw the older chick creep up behind the younger one and shove him out of the hollow with his talons. It was his father. It was his father's Special ceremony. Then he saw a flutter of white, a white that rivaled the moon. It was his mother. *You did it, Kludd. You did it. So young, but you did it. Come with us!* It was his father's Special ceremony many years ago. So he had proved his worth by trying to murder his only brother.

Nyroc swiveled his head around to his mother and fixed her with the fiercest gaze he could muster. "Mum, I will not do this. No matter what."

"No matter what?" screeched Nyra. She spread her wings, lowered her head, and began to speak in a cold, deadly voice. "Not even if I kill you?"

"Fly! Fly! Save yourself! I'm not worth it!" Phillip cried out.

"He's right, Nyroc," his mum said. "The stinking little Sooty is not worth it."

"Everyone is worth something," Nyroc replied. His own tone surprised him. His voice suddenly sounded very grown up.

Nyra looked surprised. Uglamore began to speak. "General Mam, perhaps there might be a better way. . . ."

Nyra wheeled about. "Get out of here, all of you. I must speak to my son in private."

Uglamore spread his wings to take flight. Stryker, Doc Finebeak, and the other officers followed.

When they had risen well overhead and began to dissolve into a cloud bank, Nyra turned to Nyroc.

"What of your father? Don't you love him?" she snapped.

"I never even knew him."

"Oh, you will know him very well, my dear, if you do not complete your Special. The scroom of your father shall haunt you and hunt you wherever you go until the end of your days!"

Nyroc felt himself wilf. He swung his head from his mum to Phillip and then back to his mum again. "No," he said firmly.

That simple word enraged Nyra more than anything else. She flew at her son. He tried to back off but her talon tore across his face. He felt a searing pain.

"Fly, Nyroc, fly!" Phillip shreed. His voice was filled with agony.

Then Nyra stopped and looked at her son, aghast. "What have I done? What have I done?"

Nyroc looked down. Blood was dripping on his talons. In a dazed voice, suddenly sickeningly sweet, Nyra said, "Darling child, that was not the way it was supposed to be. Not your blood. Not yours." Then her feathers fluffed up; her dark eyes turned wrathful. In less than a second she was flying full force at Phillip. Nyroc was in a yeep state, unable even to lift his wings. But it would have made no difference. It was too late. Nyra moved like lightning. Phillip lay dying at her talons.

"What have you done?" Nyroc hopped over to Phillip, whose head was at an odd angle. His eyes were filmy and there was a deep gash in his chest. Gasping for every breath, he whispered hoarsely to Nyroc, "Fly, Nyroc, fly."

Nyra plunged her talons into Phillip's chest and ripped out his heart.

"I hate you!" Nyroc shreed at his mother.

"No, you don't, my dear. You'll get over this." Nyra was speaking rapidly in a breathy voice. "This is going to be our little secret. We're going to pretend that you killed Dustytuft, not me."

He glared at his mother. For the first time he saw her shrink back a bit. He had to get out of there. He had to fly straightaway even though he was missing half his tail feathers and the wound on his face was still oozing blood.

"It will be our secret, Nyroc." She spoke with a desperation he'd never heard before. "You passed your Special ceremony. Isn't that great? So we cheated a little. I know you would have done it, given a little more time."

"You . . . know . . . nothing!" Nyroc said, slowly enunciating each word.

"Nyroc, you are my world. My entire world."

"If I am your world, it is a world I do not want to live in."

He then spread his tattered wings and flew. He clamped his beak shut against the pain of flying so nearly featherless. But he felt his will surge through his gizzard. *So this is free will?* he thought. *It hurts!*

# CHAPTER TWENTY

## *Away*

Nyroc was utterly and completely alone. He had no idea what he was flying toward. He knew only what he was flying away from: away from the rocky burnt-up canyonlands, away from the Pure Ones, away from his mother and the bloody scene that still boiled in his brain. He flew into the windless folds of the black night, wrapped himself in its cool silky darkness. He was weak, very weak, and he knew he could not fly far with his tattered feathers. But he had to fly just far enough. *Just far enough to get away.* The words played over and over like a chant in his head.

He looked down. *Those are trees,* he thought. *And perhaps if it were not night, I would see the green.* But the tall timbers that poked at the sky seemed to be fringed in black needles. *Yes, needles,* Nyroc reminded himself. *It's winter. The leaf trees would have molted. Phillip had explained what leaf trees did in the winter.*

*Phillip!* He felt his gizzard lurch with despair. He could not think of Phillip now. *Just think of away. Just think of away.*

*Perhaps that is the Shadow Forest beneath me. It can't be The Barrens for there are hardly any trees in The Barrens. Phillip said* — He cut off the thought.

Suddenly, Nyroc knew that he could not flap his wings a moment longer. He had to light down somewhere. He began circling. It was difficult. His ruddering was off. He gave the command to his tail but it just wouldn't respond as it had in the past. The trees were dense. He had heard that trees had hollows. Maybe he would find one. Maybe not. He'd settle for anything right now. He suddenly saw a bright reflection like a silver blade split the night. *It's the moon come down to earth! No, of course not. It is the moon's reflection. It must be a pool, a pond, a lake!* He had heard about such things. Nyroc began a gradual dive toward the forest pool.

He lighted down on a log on the pebble beach. A thin skin of ice had begun to form over the water. He crept toward the edge and looked down. There was still a patch of water left and when he looked and saw his own reflection he gasped. A seam ran diagonally down his face just like his mum's except that his slanted from left to right down his face, while his mum's had gone from right to left. His scar was still red with the blood that had caked in the seam. A shiver ran through his gizzard. *I am exactly like my mum!*

And at that instant, two things happened. From the

middle of the lake a mist rose. It began to swirl into a vague shape. *It's a mask! A metal mask!* Then it was as if Nyroc had stepped out of his own body and was hovering over the lake, and yet when he looked down, his talons were dug firmly into the pebbles of the beach. Could he be in two places at once? *Impossible!* But inside his head he could hear a voice, a voice he did not recognize, calling to him. *Come here, lad. Come here. Nod pule.* He saw something like his own shadow moving out from him. It was going toward the swirling shape. *Toward the scroom of my father.*

*Yes, lad. It is I. Like your mum said. There is no escaping your destiny. You must go back, Nyroc.*

*You're here on unfinished business,* Nyroc said without speaking.

*It is your business to finish, lad.*

*What is that business?*

The mask glared at him and became mute.

*I am not on earth to finish your business. I have free will.*

*Ha-ha! Ha!* the mask exploded in harsh clanking laughter that made Nyroc's gizzard shudder.

So his mother had been right. He would be haunted by his father's scroom wherever he went for the rest of his life. He was almost too weary and scared to think. How could he go on? He wanted to weep.

*Yes, how can you go on?* The scroom's echo of his thought

rang in his brain and clanged in his gizzard. *How can you do anything?*

*What do you mean?*

*To be a Barn Owl, Nyroc, is to be the noblest of birds. In your condition, frightened and nearly featherless, you are barely an owl and far from noble.*

*Maybe I should return* . . . The words were just forming in his mind when the echo clanged again.

*Yes, maybe you should return.*

*No, no, never. How can I even think of that?* He shook his head. This was not his voice speaking. It was the scroom's voice that had insidiously seeped into his head.

*To return or not. That is the question, my son.*

*No it isn't,* Nyroc replied.

*It is. It is a noble thing to be a Barn Owl, but nobler by far to be a Pure One.*

Then Nyroc suddenly remembered what Phillip had said to him when he had first begun to molt in that fox's den and was so scared. *You are more than just feathers,* he had said. So he spoke in the strange silent way of the scrooms to his father. And, as he found the courage to speak, the burnished battle claws of the great warrior were no longer his inspiration. He saw something else in his mind's eye. It was the dimly pulsating outline of a tree on an island in the middle of a vast sea. But it was more than just a tree on an island. It was a place where truth and nobility resided. Gwyndor was right when he had said that *belief is found within, in one's gizzard, in one's heart, in one's mind. It has no value if it is simply ordered like a command.* So he turned to face the weirdly glaring mask of his father's scroom.

*I am more than just feathers. I am brains and gizzard. It was not feathers that spoke to those crows. It was not feathers that figured out how to bargain with them and get a free passage.*

*What are you nattering on about, lad? Even featherless it would be nobler to remain a faithful son and suffer the demands of this great and passionate Union of Pure Ones. You are pathetic! Yeepish!*

There was a deafening clamor in Nyroc's brain. His gizzard quaked with fear and despair. But once again he roared back into the silent channels of the scrooms.

*I am not pathetic. I am not yeepish. My best friend has been murdered by my own mother. There is no question! I will not return — ever. Perhaps it would be nobler if I pick up battle claws and raise them against the Pure Ones. Yes, fight them!*

Then, suddenly, he realized he was back in his own body, the voice was gone, and the mask was dissolving into the night. Nyroc looked down. He was in exactly the same place at the edge of the lake. But he was badly shaken.

Nyroc decided to take inventory of his state, feather-wise. He peered once again at his face in the black mirror of the lake. The bloody mark left by his mother's talons was still there. No scroom had made that. It was real. He sighed. Several of the very small darker feathers that ringed his facial disk had molted. He needed to examine the rest of himself. He began stepping slowly in a small circle so different parts of his body would be reflected in the dark water that was illuminated by the rising moon. He cocked and swiveled his head. *Well, forget the plummels — they're history,* he thought. *I must be the noisiest flier around. . . . Oh, Great Glaux, is there an undertail covert left? No wonder I had trouble ruddering in for this landing. . . . All the primaries seem to be there. . . . But, uh-oh, what happened to the number eleven secondary feather?*

That was another thing Phillip had taught him — counting — along with some letters that he had scratched in the dirt with his talons. Phillip could count only up to nineteen, because owls, at least Barn Owls, had nineteen feathers on each wing. The first ten going inward from the tip of their wings were the primaries. Feathers eleven through nineteen were the secondaries. Anything beyond nineteen, Phillip said, was higher mathematics. But he had told Nyroc that the Guardians of Ga'Hoole owls knew all about higher mathematics. They were the smartest owls in the entire owl universe. *But, hey,* thought Nyroc. *I've got all my primaries. What am I complaining about?* The primaries were the most important feathers of all, the power feathers that thrust a bird forward. He pivoted around some more and observed his image in the black water. *And I've got most of my facial feathers, missing just one secondary. Yes, and several coverts, but I've still got wings. I'm an owl, I can fly — sort of.*

He promised himself that he would not whine and, like some little owl chick, say "no fair." In that moment, Nyroc realized that although he had many more feathers to grow, he, in the course of this one night, between the time he had hurled himself into the Shredders until now, had grown up.

He was not yet six months old, but his childhood was gone. He was a hatchling no more, an owl chick no more. He was a grown owl, with or without his feathers, and a member of a noble avian species, despite his mum and da.

Nyroc knew that he must lie low, literally, and wait quietly and patiently for his feathers to grow in. He thought he was most likely in some owl's territory, and he knew that owls did not like their air and their earth invaded by other owls. So although Nyroc longed to live in a hollow like the ones in the great trees of Silverveil Phillip had described, he must settle for a ground nest. If any small rodents skittered across this pebbly beach he would certainly hear them, but with winter set in — even now it had begun to snow — he could not count on bugs.

A tree on a high bank of the pond had toppled in a

previous storm. Its entire root base had been yanked up ferociously by the force of the winds. In a kind of limping flight that hardly got him off the ground, Nyroc went over to see if it might offer any refuge for a very tired and tattered owl.

# CHAPTER TWENTY-ONE
## A Fallen Tree

The tree, in fact, offered Nyroc a variety of cozy nesting spots. In the huge exposed root-ball were snug little pockets heavy with clots of dirt and dangling twisted roots. In the thick trunk itself there were several hollows and smaller holes, none of which seemed to be occupied at the moment. He had worried that one of these spaces might make a nice den for a fox, and he certainly wasn't up to taking on a fox. He had half hoped he might find a chipmunk, or a smallish rat, in one — he definitely was hungry.

But more than hungry, he was tired. So just as the light began to shred the night, Nyroc settled down into a hollow that was halfway up the fallen trunk. He was so tired, he did not even realize that he had fallen asleep on a cushion of moss, the very same kind of moss that Phillip had once described to him, the softest to be found in a forest — rabbit's ear moss.

By the time Nyroc awoke the next evening, the world

had turned white and the pond had disappeared entirely under a blanket of deep snow. His first thought was *food*! He was starved. But the sounds that he had fallen asleep with, the creaking of the trees in the wind, the clicks of a small creature's paws on the pebbles of the beach, seemed distant, almost erased by the snow. How would he ever hunt for anything in the thickness of this silence? How would he even hear the skitterings of a mouse or a vole?

He stepped cautiously out of his hollow and blinked. He was very cold with so few feathers, but he was also very hungry. Then he did hear something, a very small sound coming from the inside of the tree. He quickly stepped back into the hollow and listened. It was a crispy, creeping sound, an insect of some sort. But it was so cold, how could there be any bugs alive? Then he realized that inside this tree trunk it was not cold at all. Despite his nearly featherless condition, as he slept he had not been cold. As he was realizing this, an odd-looking thing crept right by his beak. He snapped it up before he had time to even know what he was eating. It was crunchy on the outside and soft in the middle. Yum! He swallowed it whole and immediately felt his hunger lessen. Then to his wonder, another one crept by. He snapped it up and scratched with his talon at the small opening it had come from. The wood seemed to be completely rotten and riddled with passageways that tunneled through the tree. Hadn't Uglamore once told him that nothing was better than a good old rotten tree for food? And sure enough, inside the rotted trunk, there was a veritable feast of insects and worms and all variety of creepy-crawly things that he did not even know the names for, but they would certainly satisfy his hunger.

Maybe his luck was finally turning. This uprooted massive and rotted tree was Glaux-sent. Bugs and worms were not as hearty fare as good bloody meat but he felt his energy coming back quickly and perhaps, he thought, when he had regrown enough feathers he would be able to go out and really hunt. And maybe by that time the snow would have melted.

He ate and slept and rested. And for now he felt safe.

Every day Nyroc grew stronger. He spent a great part of his time thinking, and although he was quite comfortable in the rotten tree trunk, well fed and warm, there was one incontrovertibly sad fact of his life. He was alone — completely alone. He thought a lot about this. The only friend he had ever had was dead. Although Phillip had never spoken the word "love," the Sooty must have loved him, for he was willing to die for him. And did — murdered by Nyra, who in her very strange way claimed to love him. How could love appear in so many different ways? Did Nyra really believe that she loved him?

And what of Soren? Had his uncle Soren still loved the brother who had tried to kill him for his own Special ceremony? Is that why Soren had hesitated in the cave during their last battle?

What was this thing called love? Was it knowing another being so well and trusting what you knew? A kind of believing in someone? Not believing because someone told you to, but believing because you discovered that belief in your gizzard, your heart, your mind, as Gwyndor had said? *Yes, belief and love might be wings of the same pair*, Nyroc thought. But there was one thing about love that he was sure of and that was that love was stronger than hate. It had been Phillip's love for him that made him defy his mother. It had been his love for Phillip that had made him say he would never return to the Pure Ones. And perhaps it was love, or the promise of it, that drove him on in his quest for truth that seemed to be leading to his uncle Soren. Whatever love was, it had a power beyond anything he'd ever imagined.

Nyroc settled into his hollow and his daily diet of bugs. He hid from all other owls, afraid that Nyra had sent scouts out looking for him. He feared spies, too, who might fly to the Pure Ones with news of him. So he became a most unnatural owl — sleeping by night and hunting by day.

As Nyroc huddled in the tree trunk, each day waiting for dawn when he could emerge to hunt, he would hear owls returning at dawn from their own night's hunting. He liked this time of the day for he could overhear the pleasant domestic sounds of families preparing for sleep and eating their breaklight meal. Sometimes he would leave his hollow and venture near an owl family and hide behind a tree or bush to listen in. He liked the racket of the young chicks as they were promised a story if they ate all their vole or mouse, and then were coaxed to sleep.

It was during those short hours between the last of the night and into the breaking of the dawn that he first heard the legends of Ga'Hoole. There was one he had been able to catch only fragments of. He wanted so much to hear it all for it was about King Hoole. At first, it had made him very nervous. For hadn't his mother said that not since the ancient King Hoole had there been such an owl as himself? He was intrigued and frightened by the notion of Hoole. It seemed as if a winter storm would start to brew, setting the limbs creaking, and soon the words of the story would be blown away like the old dry leaves flying by. But finally there came a still night when Nyroc heard more of the story he had learned was called the Fire Cycle of the Ga'Hoolian legend.

*It was in the time of the endless volcanoes. For years and years, in the land known as Beyond the Beyond, flames scraped the sky, turning clouds the color of glowing embers both day and night. Ash and dust blew across the land. It was said to be a curse from the Great Glaux on high. But there was a blessing hidden in the curse, for this was the time when Grank, the first collier, was hatched. This was the time when a few special owls discovered that fire could be tamed....*

The story went on to describe how Grank, a Whiskered Screech, learned how to make all sorts of tools and weapons using the different kinds of coals spewing from the volcanoes. Grank learned all there was to know about fire, flames, coals, and embers. He not only learned about the glowing parts of the volcanoes but the peculiar drafts of air that swirled about them and the pockets of poisonous gases that could instantly kill a bird or any animal that was trapped in them. The collier Grank thought he had seen every flame, fire, coal, and ember a volcano could spew forth from its cone, until one night in the dead of winter in a swirling blizzard, he saw an amazing sight. The snow lay thick on the ground. The volcano that had just erupted was not an especially large or powerful one. All of the coals had been extinguished immediately upon falling into the deep snow. All except one. This coal was strange in appearance. As she was telling the story to the young'uns the mother owl's voice suddenly grew soft and mysterious. Nyroc strained to hear from his hiding place. *"The coal, like many coals, was orange but at its center there was a most unusual color, a deep sapphire blue. Grank peered closer still and saw that rimming the blue was a brilliant, dancing edge of green. This nugget of fire came to be known as the Ember of Hoole."*

Nyroc's eyes grew wide. He felt his gizzard grow still. Were these not exactly the same colors that he had seen in the flames of Gwyndor's fire at the Marking of his father's Final ceremony? But just at that moment one of the chicks did something bad. There was a mad fluttering in the hollow, and then a squeaky little voice cried, "It got away!" The mother began scolding. "I've told you a thousand times. Don't play with the bug before you eat it. No more snacks before sleep for you. Playing with your food is vile, disgusting behavior. Cruel. Only the Pure Ones play with their food."

Nyroc cringed in his hiding place. It was true. He had watched the lieutenants and even his mum toss a dying rat about, the blood spattering everywhere before it was finally eaten. He never saw the fun in such sport, but he had never thought of it as wrong or even cruel.

"But, Mum," whined another, "finish the story, please."

*Please!* Nyroc thought. *Please finish the story.*

"It's a very long story, young'uns. It will take many days to finish it. Now, all of you to bed. Tomorrow is Eddie's first Hunt-in-Snow ceremony. He must be rested up."

"Yes, I have to be rested. Hunting in snow is very difficult."

*Don't I know it,* thought Nyroc, *and I didn't even have anyone to tell me how to do it.* Once more, Nyroc felt himself awash with feelings of loneliness. How he missed Phillip. Often when he was overwhelmed with feelings of loneliness, he dreamed of his friend. They were always wrenching dreams in which Nyra was starting her attack on Phillip, and Nyroc was frozen to the ground, his featherless wings heavy as stones, unable to do a thing to help his best friend. That, of course, was what had really happened. He had dreamed it again last night and was exhausted but now, as day was breaking, he must soon be out at this most unnatural of times for an owl to start his daylight hunting. Such were the facts of his lonely hidden existence in this forest.

But on this morning, Nyroc gave a mighty yawn and before he knew it he was fast asleep again as the night leaked steadily out of the breaking morning and bright harsh sunbeams poured in through the holes and cracks of the rotten stump. And Nyroc did dream, but not of Phillip.

He dreamed of an owl he had never seen. She was a Spotted Owl. She was perched on a limb of what could only be the Great Ga'Hoole Tree. It was an immense tree. He had never seen one larger, and he could swear it was near a sea because he could almost feel the salty breezes. She seemed to be weeping. She seemed almost as lonely as he was. But not quite. No, there was a misty shape hovering about her, which he sensed was another Spotted Owl, but an elderly one. A scroom. He heard the scroom call out softly, *Otulissa! Otulissa!* She called, but the younger owl was not listening. The elderly owl seemed to be trying to tell the younger one something. *Otulissa!* she called again. *Otulissa!*

*What a strange name*, he thought, and then the two figures merged into one vaporous cloud, and the tree itself grew misty.

Sunlight shot through the dream. Everything was dissolving into sparkling dewdrops. It was gone! Gone! Nyroc blinked his eyes open. His hollow in the old tree stump was filled with daylight. Indeed, half the day was gone. He peered out. These winter days were short and, much to his annoyance, the sun was already sliding down toward the horizon. He would be lucky if there was an hour left of good hunting before the first of the night animals began prowling for their suppers. He shook his head. The dream had been a strange one. He could hardly remember it. There had been a name spoken. He had heard it clearly, though he couldn't quite remember it. But he had not heard it as if in a dream. No, it was as if a scroom had spoken. The thought of another scroom chilled his gizzard. He stepped out of the log and listened now for the telltale scampering of small forest animals beneath the blanket of snow.

But while he hunted, he tried to remember that peculiar name, *O . . . O . . . O-tuh . . . something or other.* Every time he thought he was on the brink of grasping the name, it melted away. It seemed as hard to catch as a dewdrop on a warm sunny morning.

There were other Ga'Hoolian legends that he listened in on, stories from the Fire Cycle, the War Cycle, and one called the Star Cycle. But it was the legends of first fires and first colliers that most interested him. He wanted to know how King Hoole fit into this cycle. And he wondered what the Ember of Hoole had to do with King Hoole. It was frustrating because he caught only bits and pieces of the stories. Most annoying of all, however, was when the storyteller would say something like, "*Well, we all know what happened on that snowy night when Hoole was hatched.*"

Nyroc wanted to scream, *"No, we don't all know! Please tell the whole story!"* But, of course, he couldn't. He had to remain hidden and completely silent and alone.

Far away from the Shadow Forest, across the Sea of Hoolemere, a Spotted Owl had also been dreaming. She would not remember the dream when she woke. But as she dreamed, it seemed very real. She could almost smell the breath of the huge wolves, the ones they called dire wolves, as they loped around the cone of the volcano. They were guarding it because it held something more precious than gold, more powerful than flecks — the Ember of Hoole. But it did not make sense, of course, to guard it. "This isn't logical," Otulissa had heard herself saying to the largest wolf. "No owl can dive for this coal. They will die in the vapors and the flames. Why spend all this time guarding it?"

The wolves stopped in their tracks and dropped open their muzzles. Their long fangs flashed in the moonlight as they bayed and then the baying turned to laughter. *They're laughing at me,* she had thought. *Why are they laughing at me?* She flew down the steepest side of the volcano. She felt its shudders shake the earth. Sparks began to fly. *I have to get out of here. I'll be burned.* A coal landed on one of her coverts. She shook it off. But she could smell the odor of singed feather. She had dived into hundreds of forest fires. Retrieved all kinds of coals in her job as a collier. She had fought with fire but she had never ever been singed before.

And then that terrible image came back to her. The night Strix Struma had died in battle. One wing torn off. The other in flames as her beloved ryb and commander of the Strix Struma Strikers plummeted into the Sea of Hoolemere. In her dream, she had watched, horrified. "It's too real . . . too real," she whispered to herself as she saw the fiery bundle of feathers swallowed by the sea. Otulissa herself seemed to hang in midair, transfixed by the sea and not stirring a wing, crying for her beloved teacher. Then suddenly from the tumultuous waters, feathers spewed forth. But they were *not* the feathers of a Spotted Owl at all. Not the feathers of Strix Struma. They were buff-colored with tiny speckles of brown and then there was the terrible shree of a Barn Owl. She felt the desperation of that owl. She wanted to fly to him, but in her dream, her wings locked. She was yeep in her own dream. *This cannot be,* Otulissa protested in her dream. *I have never gone yeep in my life. Not even in battle. Never!*

When Otulissa woke up the next evening at tween time, she had no recollection of the dream but that shree and the roar of the sea still rang in her ears. But then, she thought, a winter storm is brewing in the Sea of Hoole-mere. Ezylryb had said that there was extremely nasty weather coming out of the Shadow Forest. Perhaps it had been the wind. Otulissa was a very rational bird. She did not believe in dreams. She believed in science. Even though she'd had a full day's sleep, she was awfully tired. She sensed the low-pressure front being pushed in by the foul weather and decided that it accounted for her fatigue. She reached now for one of her favorite books, *Atmospheric Pressures and Turbulations: An Interpreter's Guide.* It was written by a distinguished relative of Otulissa's, Strix Emerilla, a renowned weathertrix of the last century.

For Nyroc, on the other side of the great Sea of Hoole-mere, the nights passed and the days lengthened. The winter storms that battered the forest and took their toll on the oldest and most frail of the trees before blowing out to that immense sea became fewer. Winter grew old and the snow gradually began to melt. The sun, which had barely risen above the horizon in days, began to climb higher, a sign that winter was wearing out and spring could not be too far away. Nyroc's feathers were growing back, but he dared not go to the edge of the pond at night to look at his reflection in its black water. He still feared that the mask made of mist might swirl up from the surface and once more he would have to face the dreadful scroom of his father. So he flipped his head this way and that, pivoting his neck in fantastic swivels while counting feathers. The undertail coverts had at last all grown back, along with most of his plummels. But the cause for real celebration was when number eleven of his secondary feathers came in. Oh, how he felt like hollering and hooting. But he knew that he must remain quiet and hidden in the great rotten tree that he had come to love. Nyra might have scouts out looking for him. So instead, he made up a little song, a silly little ditty. Phillip had told him that mums often sang to their children, that his had. But Nyra had never sung to Nyroc. Even so, as spring approached, this song came to him. Someday when he was much older and had chicks of his own, he would sing it to them.

In the meantime, he sang it quietly to himself.

> There is a feather I've been told
> That helps owls fly high and bold.
> Oh, welcome back, number eleven,
> You lift me from hagsmire up to heaven.

Nyroc hopped back and forth on his feet, entertaining himself with the whispered song. The rabbit's ear moss beneath him had grown quite tattered. He had replaced some of it with another moss he had found nearby but it was not nearly so soft as the rabbit's ear moss.

Nyroc knew that soon he would have to leave the safety of the old rotted tree. He didn't know where he would go, but this part of the Shadow Forest was too close to where he had left his mother, and with the weather improving, he feared she would renew her efforts to find him. Then there was his father's scroom that he had seen again, hovering over the pond one moonlit night. No, he would have to leave. He told himself he would go when spring came. He longed to go to Phillip's hatching place — that magical and most beautiful forest of all — Silverveil.

The first shoots of spring were pushing out of the ground. On the pond, flat green leaves spread. Yes, Nyroc now knew the color green. He was entranced by it. Spring passed into summer and he still had not left. On the water, splendid pink flowers unfolded on flat, round leaves, making the pond a beautiful watery garden.

From his shelter in the rotted trunk, he had learned more than just the legends recited at daybreak. He learned about the lives of true owl families. He heard parents giving gentle scoldings and the homey lessons of kindness, and teaching something called "manners." He loved the soft lullabies the mothers crooned to their young to help them fall asleep as the night broke into day.

*Why did my mum never sing me one of those lovely lullabies?* Nyroc wondered. Just above him as the first glimmer of pink stained the sky, he heard a Boreal Owl's voice, which sounded like chimes, begin one of Nyroc's favorite stories.

*Once upon a time, before there were kingdoms of owls, in a time of ever-raging wars, there was an owl born in the country of the North Waters and his name was Hoole. Some say there was an enchantment cast upon him at the time of his hatching, that he was given natural gifts of extraordinary power. But what was known of this owl was that he inspired other owls to great and noble deeds and that although he wore no crown of gold, the owls knew him as a king, for indeed his good grace and conscience anointed him and his spirit was his crown. In a wood of straight, tall trees he was hatched, in a glimmering time when the seconds slow between the last minute of the old year and the first of the new, and the forest on this night was sheathed in ice.*

By the time the owl finished the story, Nyroc knew that the owlets, as all the other owlets in this forest, would be asleep and it would be time for him to move out in the light of day and hunt. But he dreamed of someday going to a place where he would not have to hide. But not today, not tonight. He wanted to stay just a little bit longer, here in this fallen tree that was the best home he had ever

known, with all its hollows and tunnels and plentiful supply of moss and insects of every kind.

*Not yet,* Nyroc thought. *Not yet.* Even though every single one of his feathers had grown back and he was able to
fly perfectly — *just one more day,* he thought, *one more night.*

# CHAPTER TWENTY-TWO

## The Riddle of the Forest

There is a difference between a day forest and a night forest — especially in the summer when a vast heat lies upon it and nothing seems to stir, and the air is thick with warmth and quiet. Except for the lazy hum of a bee or the occasional splash of a fish leaping in a silvery arc from a pond, a perfect silence descends upon the forest from midmorning until later afternoon.

At night, however, the forest comes alive in the coolness and the shadows. The owls come out to hunt along with the bobcat, the fox, and the raccoon. In the pond, the muskrat and the beaver leave their lodges to plow their watery paths. The grasses that grow thickly at the pond's edge shimmer with the glow of fireflies. It was a different world, a tantalizing one, which Nyroc longed to join — but he did not dare.

There was a riddle in these nights that Nyroc could not solve. Each night, almost as if to tempt him out of his hollow in the fallen tree trunk, a plump rabbit would appear just as the sun slipped beneath the horizon. The rabbit would crouch in front of a nearby shrub or small tree and not move for the longest time, staying well into the darkness and often until the moon rose high in the sky. Nyroc did not understand how this rabbit had survived. Rabbits were a favorite owl food. It seemed almost impossible that a plump one like this, standing absolutely still in a forest thick with owls, had never been preyed upon. But night after night, Nyroc watched the odd creature — hungrily, his gizzard seeming to grind in anticipation and his first stomach burbling at the thought of the rabbit's succulent flesh. Even stranger, sometimes the rabbit stood on its hind legs as if in some sort of trance.

Then one morning, after the last goodlight lullaby had been sung in a nearby fir tree, and an owl chick of a Great Gray in an oak begged for "just one more story, Da," Nyroc peered out of his hollow and blinked. There was the rabbit, standing on his hind legs almost near enough to reach out and grab. He seemed to be studying something very intently on a short branch of the fallen tree trunk. Ever so quietly, Nyroc moved out of his hollow. The rabbit was a talon's reach away. He pounced and grabbed it. Then a most shocking thing occurred. The rabbit turned its head and, looking at its would-be killer, said in a fierce voice, "Don't! Remember the vole!"

"What?" Nyroc said. He had never had a prey argue with him. Usually, if his talons had not mortally punctured it, the creature went yeep from fright and simply froze. They rarely screeched or moaned in pain. But talking? Never!

"The vole — the one you let go."

Nyroc was so astonished that he dropped the rabbit on the ground. How did this rabbit know about that vole he had left back in the fox's den in the deep canyon when the posse had shown up?

The rabbit then gave himself a little shake. "Don't worry, you didn't hurt me. Barely a scratch."

Nyroc was too stunned to speak. He felt dizzy and began to sway a bit. "Take it easy there, fellow." The rabbit extended a paw toward Nyroc's wing as if to steady him. "I don't want you crashing into my web. It's a good one. Lots of information."

Nyroc blinked several times and stared at the rabbit. It was a soft brownish-gray color, but his feet were snowy white and on his forehead there was a small white crescent of fur. Nyroc stared at him.

"That's it, fella. Take me in slowly. I am a real rabbit. But not simply dinner or tweener or breaklight, whatever you owls call your meals. There is nothing simple about me, actually. See, I can do all those rabbity things. Wanna see a cute nose twitch?" Suddenly, the velvety pink skin of his nose began to wriggle about. "Tail twitch, as well. And I can flick my ears, too. Hopping? Want me to demonstrate a hop?" He paused and looked hard at Nyroc. "Well, for Lapin's sake, say something!"

But Nyroc was speechless. Finally, he managed to say, "Who's Lapin?"

"The Big Rabbit." And he rolled his pink-rimmed eyes toward the sky. "You've got Glaux; we've got Lapin."

"Oh," Nyroc said. "But how did you know about the vole?"

"Aha! Now that's a question!" He moved closer to Nyroc. "Feeling a little steadier now?"

"Yeah, I guess so."

"Well, come over here, then." The rabbit began waddling toward the spiderweb hung between the trunk of the tree and the branch. It was a huge glittering affair, strung with jewels of morning dew.

"Beautiful, isn't it?"

"Yes," Nyroc said, although he had never thought much about spiderwebs before. A slight breeze ruffled along and the web trembled.

The rabbit suddenly froze in front of the web. "Don't

disturb me," he said in a commanding voice. Nyroc wouldn't think of it. A few minutes later, the rabbit broke out of his trance and turned to look at Nyroc.

"Just as I thought," he said.

"What? Just as you thought what?"

The rabbit then gave a kind of guffaw and slapped his pouch cheek with one foot. "Oh, silly me. I haven't explained, have I?"

"No, you haven't," Nyroc replied, his voice a little edgy. "Who are you? What are you?"

"Well, I'm a mystic of sorts," the rabbit said. "I see certain things where others don't."

"In a spiderweb?" Nyroc was awash with confusion.

"Precisely. I'm a web reader. I read spiderwebs." He tapped the crescent shape of white fur on his forehead. "This is the sign of a web reader. Only rabbits with this mark can do it. At least, as far as I know. Why do you think I've survived this long in these woods without getting eaten by something?"

"Because you're a web reader."

"That's it!"

"So, what do you see in the webs?"

"Things . . . just things," the rabbit replied elusively.

"Like me releasing the vole?" Nyroc asked.

"Yes, and other things."

"What other things?"

"In some webs I see the past, in some the present, and in some the future. But it is never a whole picture, just pieces."

"What is my future?" Nyroc said, suddenly excited. "Where am I going? What am I going to do? What will I be? Will I ever get to see my uncle Soren and the Guardians of Ga'Hoole? Will my da's scroom follow me forever?" The questions poured out of Nyroc and he wondered how he ever could have considered eating this wondrous rabbit.

"Slow down! Slow down! Didn't you hear me, lad? I said I can only see pieces of the future or the past or the present. And I don't usually know what they mean. It is as much of a puzzle to me as it is to you."

"But if you see it and tell me something, I might do it or not and that would cause things to be different," argued Nyroc.

"Not at all. I saw you release the vole. It had already happened but I saw it in the web, a rather simple one at that, a tent web, not an orb weaver's."

"Tent? Orb weaver? What are you talking about?"

"Different spiders weave different kinds of webs. You got your dome web, your orb, your tube web, your tent, your basic radial." The rabbit listed several more and then concluded, "But orb weavers are particularly rich in revealing things past. And the webs are gorgeous! Oh, my Lapin, you've never seen anything like it. But knowledge of the past or the future does not cause things to happen."

"But you said to me, 'Remember the vole,' and that made me drop you from my talons almost immediately. So it did cause something to happen."

"I wouldn't count on that." The rabbit paused and reflected a moment. "However, I did feel that you must be a very compassionate owl. For it was a very kind act when you released the vole."

"But it wasn't kind at all! I dropped the vole because the posse was coming, and Phillip told me to drop it."

"Aha! My point exactly," the rabbit said. "I told you that I only see pieces of the past or the present or the future. Apparently, the logic behind my plea for you to drop me was erroneous."

"What does that mean — erroneous?"

"Full of mistakes. Yes, the outcome was what I had hoped for, I have to admit. Sometimes it works out that way. Just pure dumb luck."

Nyroc was confused. The rabbit was answering his questions, but he felt there was much more to what he was saying. Why, for example, would he have risked standing so close to an owl's hollow, an owl who was not a dweller of this forest? And why should he have looked in that orb weaver's web and found information about Nyroc and not the many other creatures of the world? *Why me?* Nyroc wondered. *What is so special about me?* So he asked.

"Why me?"

"Why me what?" replied the rabbit.

"Why are there things about me in the webs and not other animals?"

The rabbit blinked and his pink-rimmed eyes grew sad. Nyroc saw his nose tremble a bit. He felt a tremor pass through his own gizzard. "Because your story is very important. And your story is unfinished."

"But how am I to finish it?"

"I don't know. I wish I could tell you more. But it wouldn't really make a difference."

"It might."

"No, I told you I only see pieces, and sometimes I even see those wrongly, as with the vole. I had no idea that when you released the vole, it was an act of desperation and not mercy. So I could tell you something wrong. And besides . . ." The rabbit stopped midsentence.

"Besides what?"

"You have free will. And it is only by making your own choices that the story can be finished. You already know what you must do, Nyroc. You have known since the last snows of winter melted."

Nyroc looked at him intently. "I should leave, shouldn't I." It was not really a question but a statement. The rabbit nodded silently. Several moments passed before either of them spoke. "I was thinking of going to Silverveil. It is supposed to be one of the loveliest places in the owl universe."

"Perhaps," replied the rabbit.

Nyroc had the feeling that the rabbit did not quite approve of his choice. The two animals were silent for a long time. Then Nyroc broke the silence. "How do you know my name?"

The rabbit gave a small shrug. "Oh, names are the easiest part of web reading. I get names all the time. Sometimes, however, it's hard to match up the name with the creature."

"Have you ever read the name Soren in your web?"

"Nope."

Nyroc sighed. He was disappointed. "Maybe Uncle Soren?" he asked.

"No again. But a name did show up this morning in this web here." The rabbit cocked his head toward the glistening strands that the spider had woven.

"What was it?" Nyroc asked excitedly.

"Fengo," he replied.

"'Fengo'? Is it an owl?"

The rabbit shrugged again, but this time it was an I-don't-know kind of shrug. "Could be. Could be something else, something completely different. Could be something that you once saw."

"Me?" Nyroc wasn't quite sure what the rabbit was talking about.

"You see things in the fire, don't you, Nyroc." This also was a statement and not a question.

"You know that? No one else does."

"Oh, I think there might be someone else who knows. But it's sort of the same with you as it is with me. You see things in the fire and often they are not complete. Just like my pieces from the webs, eh?"

"Yes," Nyroc replied in a barely audible whisper. Yes, he had seen things. He remembered his first vision in the flames of the fire at his father's Marking ceremony. Beneath the hisses and snapping noises of the fire, he had heard low growling sounds and he had seen strange shapes rising in an unknown landscape with weird creatures loping across it. And then there was the odd flame with the lick of deep blue at its center and tinted at the edges with a color that he knew now was truly green. Just as he was thinking about the flame's color, the rabbit said, "Did you see Silverveil in your fire?"

"I —I'm not sure," Nyroc stammered. "Did you see it in your web?"

"Definitely not. Not even a leaf," the rabbit replied emphatically. Nyroc dared not ask him if he had seen the same strange place with the odd shapes and creatures that he had seen in the flames of Gwyndor's fires. He didn't want to hear about it if he had. "You know, Nyroc, I did not learn how to read webs instantly. I had to practice — all those different webs after all." The rabbit rattled off the names of a half dozen more kinds of webs. "As I said, it takes practice. I bet there are as many kinds of flames and coals as there are webs. You should find some fires to sharpen up your flame-reading skills. Might learn something of this future that so concerns you."

"But how would I do that? I don't know any Rogue smiths around here."

"You don't need a Rogue smith. Keep an eye out for the occasional forest fire. And, of course, there are always fires burning in Beyond the Beyond."

Nyroc started. His eyes flew open at the mention of this place. "You've heard of it?" the rabbit asked.

"Yes. I heard some of the owls telling bedtime stories about it."

"Ah, yes. From the Fire Cycle of the Ga'Hoolian legends."

"But it's just a legend, isn't it?" Nyroc said. "Just a made-up place?"

"Hardly! No, it's very real."

"You think I should go there?"

"I can't do your thinking for you, Nyroc. It's your decision. But there are lots of fires there. Extraordinary fires. It's where the first colliers came from. You want to learn about flame reading, that's the place."

"Yes, yes, I suppose so. But not quite yet. Maybe someday," Nyroc said softly.

The rabbit looked at him quizzically. "Yes, someday," he repeated, but the words sounded hollow to Nyroc, as if the rabbit did not really believe he would ever go there.

"Well, in any case, I think I should be getting along now," Nyroc said.

"Yes, it will soon be evening."

Nyroc was shocked. He had not realized that they had been talking for hours and hours and that the sun had swung low in the sky. Its long shafts of light were now piercing the branches of the trees near the ground. The pond was blazing with the violent oranges and deep pinks of a setting sun. *Yes*, Nyroc thought, *it is time for me to leave.*

The rabbit waited with him in the gathering lavender shadows of the twilight. When those shadows deepened to purple, Nyroc hopped onto the trunk of the fallen tree that had been his home for so long. He was about to say good-bye and to spread his wings but stopped.

"Rabbit, I don't even know your name. What is your name?"

"Oh, just call me Rabbit, that's good enough."

"But you must have a name," Nyroc protested.

"I do. But I can't tell you."

"Why not?"

"If I tell you, I lose my powers."

"But you said names were so easy."

"Yes. The names of others. But not one's own. Maybe you'll find my name in your fires."

Nyroc blinked.

"Good-bye, Nyroc."

"Good-bye, Rabbit."

# CHAPTER TWENTY-THREE

# A New World

Nyroc's tree stump was in the most southern portion of the Shadow Forest. He bid it good-bye with one glance over his starboard wing. In order to reach Silverveil, he flew a northeasterly course, cutting across the very top of The Barrens, which, true to its name, had scarcely a tree to perch in. He was getting awfully tired because he had been battling headwinds for hours. It was still a long time until dawn, and he thought he might set down for a rest and get a bite to eat before going on, even if that rest had to be on a boulder. Still high above the ground, he heard the skitterings of small animals, most likely rodents scampering across that hard ground. He did think that it would be a long time before he could consider rabbit as proper prey again. No. Right now he would settle for a mouse, a scrawny chipmunk, whatever.

He began carving a turn. It felt great to have his tail feathers working so well again. He alighted gracefully on a boulder and waited patiently, thinking something was bound to pass his way.

Something was. But it was not his next meal. A young Burrowing Owl emerged from a hole Nyroc had not noticed. It had been so long since Nyroc had spoken to an owl, he actually went into the frozen defense posture hoping that he would blend in with the boulder on which he perched. But such was not the case. The young Burrowing Owl saw him and froze herself, dropping the small bundle she was carrying in her beak. It was young Kalo, daughter of Harry and Myrtle. They were just preparing for the family's move to Silverveil. Harry had finally talked Myrtle into trying tree living just for the summer.

Kalo opened her eyes wide at the sight of Nyroc. *Could this really be her?* she thought, staring hard at him.

There was not a corner of the owl kingdom that had not welcomed with joy the news of the Pure Ones' defeat by the Guardians of Ga'Hoole. But it had been rumored that although the one called Metal Beak, the leader, had been killed, his mate, Nyra, was still alive. There had been sightings of her all over. Kalo looked at this owl in front of her and, though she had never seen Nyra, everything seemed to fit what she had heard of her: the face, unusually large and white for a Barn Owl, shaped more like a moon than a heart. And yes, she blinked, the scar was there, too, slashing diagonally across the face — just like the scar Nyra was supposed to have. Kalo was so frightened that she did not notice that this owl was male, not female. As far as Kalo was concerned, this was Nyra.

Finally, the Burrowing Owl gathered up her courage and spoke. "W-w-what are you doing here?"

"Just resting. I'm on my way to Silverveil," Nyroc replied.

"Silverveil," a voice from the burrow pealed out. Myrtle waddled from the opening, stopped dead in her talon tracks, and wilfed at the sight of Nyroc.

Nyroc, trying to be sociable, took a step forward. "My name is Ny —"

He never got to finish. Both owls screeched and dove back into their burrow. "She's here, Harry. Nyra is here. And she's going to Silverveil. We're not going to Silverveil. Enough of your yoickish ideas."

Nyroc listened in a dazed state to the squabbling from the burrow. His gizzard seemed numb but his mind slowly began to process what he was hearing. *They think I am my mother. They think I am a Pure One come to capture or kill them.*

Without another thought, he spread his wings and lifted off. He was half mumbling, half crying all the things he had meant to say to the Burrowing Owls, but never had the chance. "I only came for rest. I wasn't going to stay. My name is Nyroc, not Nyra. I am nothing like my mother or my father. . . ."

*But you are, Nyroc! You are!* a chorus of voices swirled in his head. *You will never escape. And no matter where you go, you shall be hated and feared. Go back to the Pure Ones. Go back. You shall be revered. You are their leader, their king.*

It was a night in which the black was thick and neither moon nor stars shone above. A glaring gray light slowly whirled around Nyroc, first on one side of him, then the other. It was not his father's scroom. It was three others — made of shreds of gray mist that appeared like tattered owls with fierce yet colorless eyes. They flew with him, one at the tip of each wing, another at his tail feathers.

They looked as if they had come from hagsmire — hagsfiends caught up in a frenzy of hag winds. These singing gray shadows whirled about him and sang out in screechy voices:

> *We are the voices of the dead.*
> *We've come to tell you what to dread.*
> *A feeble prince, you've taken flight.*
> *You shall be ours before the night.*
> *But if your gizzard gallgrot gets*
> *A king of kings it shall beget.*

The words of their gruesome song made Nyroc shiver. Were they threatening him with death — "You shall be ours before the night"? Nyroc realized that despite the violent circling of these scrooms about him, they caused no wind. Indeed, the headwind he had been battling before he had landed in The Barrens had all but vanished.

Nyroc flicked his port wing first, then his starboard one, ruddered his tail, lowered his head, and said in a very quiet voice, "You are nothing. Not even wind." And he thrust forward through the misty figures that seemed to dissolve into the night.

Yet still his gizzard quivered. Why had they followed him? Why had their voices seeped into his head?

He was more determined than ever to get to Silverveil.

# CHAPTER TWENTY-FOUR
## A Terrible Beauty

In the distance, Nyroc saw a low range of hills. His gizzard fluttered. This must be the northern border of The Barrens. Phillip had told him about these hills. Just beyond them, not far was the most beautiful part of Silverveil, a region called Blythewold. There were all sorts of owls in Blythewold, including Barn Owls of all breeds. Surely he would be welcome here. He flew faster.

Soon the hills were beneath him, and the moon had finally risen in the sky. Everything was awash in its silvery light. Oh, he knew what green was now. Never had he seen such greenness. He could hear the rippling silver sound of what seemed like a hundred brooks. A light wind stirred the sedges that grew along their banks. There were trees of all sorts. Trees with broad leaves that whispered in the breeze, some whose leaves were not green but red, and some even yellow. And trees that had no leaves at all, but long, thin, drooping branches like golden strands. These trees grew by the lakes, of which there were many, and these strands of gold swept over the surface of the water, making beautiful sighing sounds. Oh, this was where he would live forever and ever. This would be his home. He would explain who he was. That he was nothing like his mum or da, that he had left them and the Pure Ones.

Nyroc felt he was on the brink of a whole new world, a whole new life. No more day-for-night living. He would join the wonderful nighttime of owls — fly with them, hunt with them, live with them. But night was now thinning into the dawn. He would have to wait through a long day for First Black. Oh, he was so impatient!

Nyroc had decided it might be a bit forward to try for a hollow in one of these lovely trees. He didn't want to have to go poking his beak into places that might be occupied just when mums and das were trying to get their young'uns to sleep with lullabies and stories. He would be patient. He'd settle for something on the ground. And he should find it quickly. It had been exceedingly hot, and now in the dwindling night, the sky pulsed with silent flashes of light — heat lightning. The air was heavy with the smell of a summer storm about to break. He should find shelter. There were several old rotted-out stumps that would do for a day. Just one day.

He soon tucked himself into a lovely old stump, overgrown with mosses and lichen. In a tree not too far away, he had heard a mother Barn Owl begin to tell a story from the Fire Cycle. He had been sleepy, but he was suddenly alert. "You see," the mother was saying, "it was Grank, the first collier, who became the ryb for King Hoole." Hoole! He knew there was a connection. "Now, dears, you know, of course, how the legend of the coming of Hoole begins." And for once Nyroc knew what the storyteller would say next. The words were among the most beautiful of any of the legends. *Once upon a time, before there were kingdoms of owls, in a time of ever-raging wars, there was an owl born in the country of the North Waters and his name was Hoole....*

But now the mum was telling something he had never heard before. Was it part of the Fire Cycle or the Hatching Cycle stories? Her voice was lovely on this summer night. "But, young'uns, even before the great Hoole had been hatched, there were others who feared his coming. It was rumored that a hagsfiend from hagsmire had been sent to destroy the egg. The father of the hatchling Hoole had been murdered several days before the egg had hatched out. And with his dying breath, he said to his mate, 'Seek out my old ryb, Grank, and he shall know what to do. There is no choice, my dear. You must give the egg to Grank. He shall care for it and raise the chick as if it were his own. These are dangerous times.' And the mother knew that the father was right. It must be the hardest thing in the world for a mother to part with her young'un before it even hatched."

"Oh, Mum," one of the little chicks interrupted, "you wouldn't do that to us, would you?"

"If it meant you would die if I did not give you up, I would certainly do it."

Nyroc could hardly believe what he was hearing. This was a part of the cycle he knew nothing of. That Hoole was taken from his mother and raised by Grank.

"So, what happened?" said another voice. "Did the hatchling learn how to be a collier like Grank?"

"Soren's a collier, isn't he?" said another.

Now Nyroc stood straight up, as straight as he could in the cramped hollow of the old stump. *Soren . . . a collier! They're talking about Soren? My uncle.*

"Yes, so they say."

"Quit interrupting," said one of the chicks. "Tell the part about the Ember of Hoole and how Hoole found it."

"That's a story for another day, young'uns."

"Oh, no . . . please, Mum . . . just a little more . . ." They all began pleading for another little bit of the story, and Nyroc felt like joining in. The problem was that young chicks could never concentrate on anything for long so by the next dawn, they might be asking for a completely different story. It might take forever for Nyroc to hear the story of Grank and Hoole and the Ember. Especially the Ember. And he needed to. He was almost desperate in his need to hear the story of Grank and Hoole, and especially the Ember of Hoole. Somehow this story of the coal had something to do with him. He wasn't sure what, but he had to find out. He would have to wait, however. Story time was over. He yawned sleepily although it was nearly time for him to start hunting. He could see the dawn through the cracks in the rotted stump.

*Hoole is from the time of legends, and the Ember of Hoole was hidden in ancient times by the collier Grank. But Soren lives and the tree is real. Maybe,* Nyroc thought, *someday I will go to the Great Ga'Hoole Tree and meet my uncle Soren and become a collier.*

*Maybe not!* said another voice in his head. Nyroc felt his gizzard lurch. He opened one eye halfway and peered out from the hollow in the stump. A gray shadow loomed against the rising sun. The dawn wind drove the tatters of mist, which swirled, then clumped together. Nyroc felt dread in his gizzard as he saw the familiar shape of the horrible mask — first the beak, then the hollow eyes. Just as the sun slipped up over the horizon, breaking like a bloodied yolk low in the sky, the mask seemed to turn molten, a fiery red. The beak moved.

*Maybe not!* The two words thundered in Nyroc's head.

His gizzard froze, and he felt himself wilf with a terror he had never known before.

Suddenly, he heard a loud crack in the sky. Lightning crashed through the forest. There was an enormous explosion, and he heard the screech of owls fleeing from the very tree where the mum had minutes before been reciting the legend of the Coming of Hoole. And they were fleeing from other trees as well. The stump where he had taken refuge for the night was suddenly squirming with the sounds of all manner of small animals fleeing — snakes, rats, and squirrels. The snapping and sizzling of dry wood was deafening. The forest was ablaze. But Nyroc remained in the stump. He could not move once he had peeked out and saw the fire. It was as if he was hypnotized. Huge flames, immense flames reached for the moon, now merely a dim outline in the dawn sky.

Odd shapes leaped from the flames, shapes of creatures he had never seen before, or so he thought, until he saw the flash of green in the strangely tilting eyes as the four-legged creatures loped through a fiery mist in the middle of the flames. The heat was building fiercely. But Nyroc hardly felt it. The young Barn Owl was entering a state that experienced colliers knew to be the most dangerous of all. He was fire-yeep. As the fire raged with its terrible beauty Nyroc stared, transfixed by the flames. His wings hung heavily at his side. He had no thoughts of flying. He read the fire and its flames. He loved them. He could hear songs in the fire. He was the fire and the fire was he.

# CHAPTER TWENTY-FIVE
# A Legend of Coals

Grank, the first collier, was more than just a collier. He became one of the most revered rybs in Ga'Hoolian history." Otulissa spoke quietly. The Spotted Owl looked at the students who were listening to her raptly in the library of the Great Ga'Hoole Tree in a late-night predawn class. "He was, in fact, the ryb for our very first King Hoole, and you all know the story of Hoole." The little owlets nodded. Although Otulissa was a strict, no-nonsense ryb, and most of the owls were quite shy in her presence, they all loved to hear her stories of the very old days. There was a little owl who was not shy, however. She was a very inquisitive little Pygmy Owl who would never let anything stand in the way when she wanted to know something. "Yes, Fritha, you have a question?"

"Is it true that King Hoole . . . well, that they knew he was the real king for all of the owl Universe, because he found the Ember of Hoole and could hold it in his beak?"

"Well, so they say," Otulissa said. "I mean, that is part of the legend. Before King Hoole discovered it, it was called the Glauxian Coal. It was Grank, the first collier, who found it. He knew it had special powers that could be used or misused. According to the legend, he dropped it into the cone of a volcano to hide it to keep it safe. Although those first colliers could dive into volcanoes, he felt that only the noblest of owls would sense its presence there and retrieve it."

"Can colliers still dive into volcanoes? The ones who live in Beyond the Beyond?"

"Oh, no. That is an art that has been long lost. No owl has dived into a volcano in probably a thousand years."

"Not even Ruby?" Fritha asked.

The little owl was listening intently. She blinked, and the white tufts of feathers that arched over her bright yellow eyes made her look remarkably studious. Ruby was a very powerful collier. A Short-eared Owl, she was known for her spectacular flying.

"Not even Ruby," Otulissa said quietly.

"But what was the Glauxian Coal exactly?" Fritha persisted.

Otulissa continued, "The Ember of Hoole is said to be a type of bonk coal of extraordinary powers. You all know what bonk coals are?" The owlets nodded. Early on they had been told about bonk coals, which were the hottest coals that a collier could pull from a forest fire and were greatly coveted by all blacksmiths. They had many uses in the making of metal tools. "But according to legend there was only one Ember of Hoole, and when Hoole died, some say it died with him. But others say it was taken to the land of Beyond the Beyond and hidden there."

"I heard . . ." a Great Gray Owl named Buck started to speak.

"Yes, Buck, please raise a talon before speaking," Otulissa said.

Buck raised his talon and continued. "I heard that it's buried someplace there near a volcano and guarded by dire wolves."

"Dire wolves?" Fritha said. "That's stupid."

"Now, now," Otulissa cautioned. "We maintain a civil discourse here." All the owls looked blankly at her. They had no idea what "civil discourse" was, but they were pretty sure it was something about not being rude.

"Well," continued Fritha. "I only meant to say they are extinct. As in, long gone! No more!"

"We think they are extinct," Otulissa replied. When Buck had first mentioned the dire wolves there was a small twinge in Otulissa's gizzard. Something felt familiar to her, as if she had seen one someplace, but that was ridiculous. Dire wolves were thought to be extinct, and they had never been anywhere near the Island of Hoole. The only place dire wolves had ever been mentioned in connection with was the Beyond the Beyond. Even in the Northern Kingdoms, where they had wolves of all kinds, there had never been any dire wolves.

Then a Barn Owl raised its talon. "But do you think it could be true at all — not the wolf part, but the legend of the Ember of Hoole?" The young Barn Owl's black eyes shone with such enthusiasm and hope that Otulissa dearly wanted to say yes, it was true. But all she could say was, "Wensel, it could be true. No one knows for certain, but it could be true."

"Could?" Wensel repeated. "Just could?"

Otulissa nodded. She wished she could say more. It was odd but lately, since she had been teaching the young'uns about the Fire Cycle, Otulissa had been having gizzard disturbances and unsettling dreams. But Otulissa was extremely practical and did not really believe in dreams. Oh, they were all right for some owls like Soren who had starsight. But she did not consider it all that reliable. It was not scientific in the least and Otulissa was a great believer in science. She required facts, evidence, testable results.

But not only did Otulissa feel that she might have been

dreaming more lately, she also had the distinct feeling that the scroom of her old, dearly beloved ryb, Strix Struma, was somehow a part of these dreams. And Otulissa absolutely did not believe in scrooms. Not one bit. She thought they were some kind of optical illusion that grew out of a disorganized or feverish mind. But Otulissa was not disorganized and she had never had a fever, not even when she had been wounded in the great Battle of the Siege.

Otulissa did not believe that Strix Struma would even possess a scroom, let alone haunt her with it. Of all the owls in the universe, Strix Struma would not be one with an unsettled spirit. There was no possible reason for the scroom of such an owl as Strix Struma to haunt the earth. She had finished her business in this world magnificently, with valor, grace, and courage. She had led a full life.

But nonetheless, there were times of late when Otulissa had begun to wonder. And then there was the issue of the Fire Cycle. Why had she begun after all these years to see the legends in a new light? Why had they started to disturb her in some strange way? It was as if these legends had a special significance, a meaning just for her. Was she somehow reading between the lines? Was there some message encoded in these writings just for her? Each time she read them, she felt a new sense of urgency and yet despair. *Why? Why? Why?* It was as if the stories of the cycle were echoes of some long-forgotten dream she had had. Impossible. She never dreamed.

Twixt time was upon them. It would be the hour of breaklight in the dining hollow and then on to their own hollows for rest. Otulissa wasn't hungry and was not inclined to go chatting it up in the dining hollow this dawn. So, after leaving the young owlets, she retired directly to her own hollow, passing Mrs. Plithiver, the elderly nest-maid snake of Soren and Eglantine, in a hallway.

"What, no breaklight for you, Otulissa?" Mrs. P. asked.

"No, Mrs. P. I thought I'd just hit the moss."

The nest-maid's head swiveled around and followed Otulissa. Although nest-maids were blind, they were known for their refined sensibilities, and Mrs. Horace Plithiver possessed some of the most refined sensibilities imaginable. She had noticed for the last few days that Otulissa had been out of sorts and although she was only a snake — and snakes did not have scrooms — she could have sworn she sometimes felt fine, scroomish vibrations circling about Otulissa.

As the morning light filtered into the hollow, Otulissa tossed restlessly in her sleep. This was a dream, and she could not escape it. She saw fire and flames. The songs of the

Fire Cycle wove through her brain. Her gizzard twitched madly. But even in this daymarish sleepscape, Otulissa struggled to remain rational and calm. *This is just a bad dream,* she told herself. *It has more to do with indigestion than dreaming. It must have been that sugar glider they served at tweener, or the roasted bat wings. You know you can't eat roasted bat wings, Otulissa!* she scolded herself in her sleep. *It always upsets your stomachs — both of them. I must go tell cook not to take offense if I don't eat the bat wings. I do love that barbecue sauce, though.*

Only Otulissa would think of apologizing to the cook in the midst of a bad dream!

When the dream finally ebbed, and she at last escaped into sleep for the few hours of the day that were left, it was still not a peaceful sleep. And when she rose before tweener, she felt completely exhausted and for the first time ever she could almost remember the blurry outlines of her dream. She peered at herself in the fragment of looking glass. "Great Glaux, I look a sight!" she muttered. Well, perhaps a good tweener would set her up. Thank goodness, she had her lesson prepared for the young'uns. But then she remembered what the lesson was: the Fire Cycle, part two. "Racdrops," she swore softly. Otulissa hardly ever swore, but she was definitely not inclined to discuss the Fire Cycle this evening. She had had enough of it during her turbulent sleep.

# CHAPTER TWENTY-SIX

## The Spirit Woods

O tulissa! That is the name! Her name is Otulissa."
And with that, Nyroc broke from his hollow, which
had become thick with smoke in the blazing forest. He
rose through the columns of flames, finding drafts on
which he could surge upward. And although this young
owl had never been trained as a collier, he had all of the
instincts of one. He rode the hot spires of air that sliced
like knives through the night. He had a natural sense of
where the air suddenly cooled to what colliers called a
"dead drop," which could drag an unobservant owl straight
down to the ground.

Then an ember whizzed by and he caught it in midflight, an amazingly difficult feat that took most colliers
many seasons of experience in forest fires to master. If an
old collier had seen him, he would have exclaimed, "By
Glaux! You'd think he'd been trained by Grank himself."
For indeed, he had what was often called a Grankish style

of flight, slicing the air with wings hunched slightly forward and angled down. This was called the "reverse Grank sheer" and could help a collier spin around the fringe of a rising crown of embers and snap off the best ones.

But it was all instinct with Nyroc. He did not even know the terms for what he was doing as he flew through the flames — reverse Grank sheers, catching the ember crowns. No, he was not even thinking about this. He was looking down into the flames and thinking about the Spotted Owl named Otulissa. Once she had dissolved from his dream like dewdrops in the morning sun, but now he could almost see her, feel her. At first, he was sure it was she and she was calling to him. But then he realized it was another Spotted Owl, an elderly one. And he saw the image of this older one clearly now in the flames. Could she be a scroom? He had never heard of a good scroom before. But this one he could trust. He sensed it deep in his gizzard. He was seeing her in the flames. He was reading her. She was no hagsfiend, no hagsmire-bent scroom. No, this scroom was all goodness, glaumora-sent.

*Follow me! Follow me!* the scroom's voice sounded in his brain.

He looked down. The fire had vanished, but the voice guided him on. Indeed, he was no longer in Silverveil.

They were northeast of Silverveil. He could see the Sea of Hoolemere. Was she taking him to the Island of Hoole, to the Great Ga'Hoole Tree?

*No.* The clipped but kindly voice filled his head.

He looked down. They were flying over a peninsula and beneath them was a very strange forest. Nyroc had not seen many trees or forests in his short life, but even he could tell this one was most peculiar. All the trees had white bark and not one tree had a single leaf on it. It was a dark and moonless night. But it might as well have been day, for this forest with its white-barked trees seemed to glow. Then within the glow of these woods an eerie intensity gathered into a luminous shape. And within that luminosity there were brighter points of light that twinkled with a shimmering beauty. The luminous shape rose until Nyroc realized that hovering before him in midair was the Spotted Owl he had read in the flames and whose voice had guided him to this strange place. She was composed entirely of light. He felt himself float down from where he had been flying and perch on some invisible branch in the ghostly woods.

*What is this place?* he asked.

*A spirit wood,* came the answer. Once again, the voices, his own and that of the scroom, could not be heard aloud but remained sealed in his head. Nyroc felt a dim tweak of fear pulse through his gizzard. *It is a scroom!*

*But not like the one who has haunted you. This is a spirit wood and a spirit wood will not harbor evil scrooms. It is the only place the evil ones cannot enter.*

*But why are you here? Why am I here?* Nyroc asked.

*We must wait.*

*Wait for whom?* Nyroc silently asked.

*I think you know.*

*I do?*

*Think, Nyroc, think.*

*Otulissa?*

The scroom nodded. *You saw her in the flames, didn't you? She will help you complete your journey.*

*But what is my journey?*

*I cannot tell you that. You must find that out for yourself.*

*But what am I to do? And if I must find it out for myself, why should Otulissa come here?*

*To and from,* the Spotted Owl said cryptically, and her spots twinkled with such intensity that Nyroc had to blink. It was as if he were looking directly into the sun.

*To and from?* he asked. But the scroom did not reply. *But what am I to do?*

The scroom took a long time before she answered. *You*

*know what you must do. I was hoping that she would come here to help guide you. But she is a stubborn one. Her head often gets in the way of her gizzard. She cannot believe what she cannot see or prove.*

But what of the dire wolves? Nyroc was surprised by his own words.

*Yes, exactly. So, you know about them. You saw them in the flames, didn't you?* the scroom asked, and Nyroc nodded. He hadn't realized until this moment that those loping creatures with the slanting green eyes he had seen in the flames were actually dire wolves.

*She doesn't believe in them or in dreams or in scrooms.*

Nyroc knew she was speaking of the owl named Otulissa.

*But you know scrooms exist, don't you, young'un?*

Nyroc nodded. *This has something to do with the Ember, the Ember of Hoole, doesn't it? And something I must do.*

But the glowing scroom of Strix Struma had begun to fade. The spots twinkling just seconds before seemed to blur. *Watch for her, Nyroc,* the scroom said. *Watch for Otulissa.*

Now a fog bank rolled in from the Sea of Hoolemere and enfolded the luminous shape into its thick roiling vapors. She was gone. Nyroc felt something slide together within the deepest part of his gizzard. There was a soft jolt as one part of his being rejoined the other. He peered down. The toes of his talons were wrapped firmly around the white limb of a tree.

He looked to where the fog bank had rolled back out to sea. Did he hear a thin voice whispering to him, "*Glaux-speed, young'un*"?

# CHAPTER TWENTY-SEVEN
## Dire Wolves

It was midafternoon at the Great Ga'Hoole Tree when Otulissa entered the library. The entire tree was sound asleep. She picked this time to do her research because she didn't want anyone sticking their beaks into her business. But she aimed to find out all she could about dire wolves. Were they just the stuff of legends or had they ever truly existed? It seemed strange to her that books on both legends and science were next to one another on the shelves. She didn't quite approve. In Otulissa's well-organized mind, the two were entirely separate divisions of knowledge. One had nothing to do with the other. One could be proven through experimentation; the other could not. Yet both were valuable for exercises in the development of the mind and gizzard. Their purposes were different: The intent of science was to give insight to the natural history of the earth and its creatures. The purpose of legend was to challenge the imagination and develop the finer sensibilities of the gizzard.

She opened the first book, entitled *Four Leggeds: Ancient*

*and Extinct,* written by a highly respected Burrowing Owl of the previous century. Burrowing Owls, perhaps because of their digging abilities, had led the field in the study of fossilized bones. Otulissa settled down to read, and her attention was immediately attracted to the drawing of an immense tooth larger than any canine fang she had ever seen.

"My, my," Otulissa muttered. The tooth was as long as her own leg!

*The dire wolf,* the text stated, *is far more robust than its cousin the ordinary wolf, Canis lupus.*

"I would say so!" Otulissa softly exclaimed.

*Although similar in many ways to a large modern gray wolf, the dire wolf had a larger, broader head. The most obvious differences to its modern-day relative were its massively sturdy legs. Despite being shorter than a gray wolf's legs and perhaps not as good for running, they were excellent for pouncing and bringing down prey. This characteristic, coupled with enormous teeth capable of crushing bones, made the dire wolf of ancient times a formidable predator. It has furthermore been speculated that because of its larger and broader head, it possessed a great brain as well.*

*Although no expeditions have been sent into the territory known as Beyond the Beyond at this date, some scholars maintain that large migrations of wolves went there eons ago at about the same time sheets of the last great ice covered much of the earth. It was this ice age that was accountable for the extinction of many large carnivores. Most scholars agree it is doubtful that any dire wolves could have survived.*

"Well, dead is dead," Otulissa said, "and extinct is even more dead than dead."

"So they say," a voice croaked from behind a high stack of books.

Otulissa was so startled that she rose up in a sudden hover from where she had been perched reading.

"Ezylryb!" she exclaimed. The ancient ryb of the great tree had been concealed behind his stack of books.

"What are you doing here?" she asked.

"I might ask the same of you," he replied.

"Oh, I'm just reading up on dire wolves. They're extinct, you know."

"So they say," he repeated.

"No, they really are!" Otulissa said forcefully.

"Extinct perhaps in books of science but, of course, poetry, literature, and legends are timeless. Is it not the purpose of legends to transcend the humdrum rhythms of our lives, the ordinary, crude borders that confine us to the present, that we may live instead in the ever-gleaming light of knowledge? I direct you to the third canto of the second book of the Fire Cycle, lines 47–99." The old ryb, now almost as white with age as a Snowy, raised his foot to point, the same foot with only three talons that had so intimidated Otulissa when she had been a youngster.

"Yes, sir, I have a copy of the Fire Cycle in my hollow. I think I'll read it there."

The words Ezylryb had spoken had deeply agitated Otulissa. Ezylryb was known for his devotion to science, but here he was saying that she should go read the Cycles — as if this would provide evidence of dire wolves. She could not shake the feeling that Ezylryb was aware of the deeper disturbance in her — which had something to do with the dreams that had been robbing her of sleep. Well, if she was going to read these legends she would prefer to do so in the privacy of her own hollow. So she returned there. The sun was still well above the horizon. There was ample time until tweener and night flight.

When she entered the hollow, it seemed chilly although it was the middle of summer. She poked at the almost dead coals in the grate of her fireplace. As a full-fledged Guardian and ryb, she was allowed a hollow with a coal grate, which was quite nice for chilly days. Then she noticed that she had stirred up some dust. She hated any kind of untidiness. She supposed she could call for a nest-maid snake but it would be easy to clean up herself. Otulissa found one task after another to do. But she finally realized that she could no longer avoid the real task awaiting her. The pursuit of knowledge was a noble one, yes, almost sacred. Only cowards and fools shunned it. So she went directly to her bookshelf and reached for her old tattered copy of the Fire Cycle and picked through it gently with her talons. She found the canto and the verses that Ezylryb had told her about and began reading.

*And in the whisper of moon's last light*
*The dire wolf, Fengo, traversed the night.*
*And then another and still another followed him,*
*Until a pack across the earth did roam*
*Ever onward to seek a warmer home.*
*Bereft of hope and gnawed by hunger,*
*They sought a better place to dwell.*
*Far from the ice-locked country whence they came,*
*Far from the coldness that was their hell.*

*And each time a wolf did ask, "Where will this journey end?"*
*Fengo, their leader, did reply, "Just beyond the yonder. There!*
*See those fires that scorch the sky*
*Beyond the mountains that scrape the air?*
*See the blackness that bleeds hot coals*
*And makes the darkness shine with light?*
*Where fires turn the moon bloodred,*
*These same fires melt snow and ice*

*And leave the land unlocked, undead.*
*Beyond the next beyond!" Fengo's howl the air did rend.*
*The wolves howled in return, "Will this journey never end?"*
*Yet end it did and in its end a new beginning now was found.*
*And thus did Fengo and his wolves come to this land beyond beyond.*
*Beneath the fiery cones they made their den.*

*In rocks and caves of black mountains*
*That glittered with shards of volcanic glass,*
*Between the coal fields and fires they came to dwell.*
*This was their heaven and not their hell.*
*And with that fire monster they made amends.*
*Yet in that place beyond beyond*
*Many others met their ends.*

Otulissa read on. She had known about the time of the great ice sheets. It had caused a mass extinction among large animals, and it had taken thousands of years for life to regenerate itself. But smaller creatures had somehow managed to survive. Many of the most desperate of these sought their way, like the dire wolves, to Beyond the Beyond. It seemed that since history began desperate creatures have been drawn to Beyond the Beyond and made its inhospitable landscape their home. Even in the present day, it was known that a lot of hire claws lived there.

The next canto was very poetic and one of Otulissa's favorites. It went on to describe how Grank hid the Ember of Hoole to keep it safe. She loved the rousing lines that came next, telling of Grank's rescue of the hatchling Hoole:

> *In the darkness of that same night,*
> *Another came in desperate flight*
> *To rescue the prince now called Hoole*
> *Sent to end the wars so cruel.*

Then came the last canto, the meaning of which was still being argued by scholars. Otulissa read slowly, carefully.

> *So bring him back with flames of gold.*
> *Bring him back with burning fire.*
> *For he reads what flames have told,*
> *And his will is Hoole's desire.*
> *He shall not cease his endless flight.*
> *He shall fly on through days and nights.*
> *Though an outcast in despair,*
> *He has a gizzard that is so fair.*
> *He shall return at summer's end,*
> *Coal in his beak, a shadow king no more,*
> *Tempered wise and brave for war.*

Otulissa stopped reading. *How can this be?* she wondered. She reread the last stanza. There had always been talk of missing cantos near the end of the Fire Cycle. It was felt that lines might have been lost. There were some scholars who insisted that the last stanza was a prophecy and that the missing materials would support this. Otulissa had always dismissed this as second-guessing. But when she read this last stanza yet again, it now seemed to be talking about another owl, not Hoole at all, as she had always thought. *For he reads what flames have told, And his will is Hoole's desire.* It was as if Hoole was speaking of another owl. Was Hoole making a prophecy?

Otulissa felt a shiver run through her own gizzard. The light in her hollow was dim despite the sun outside the opening that heralded a clear sunny morning. Goodness! She had read by candlelight all through the night and into the next morning. She had completely missed night flight. She was about to blow the candle out but stopped a moment to sleepily watch its flickering flame dancing on the wall of the hollow. She knew that there were some owls who were said to be fire readers. Was that what this poem in the Fire Cycle was about? Was Hoole foretelling the coming of a flame reader?

*Yes,* a familiar voice whispered in her head.

Otulissa blinked. *Strix Struma?*

The candlelight cast a large shadow that stretched high against the wall of her hollow. As she looked up, the shadow seemed to be gathering together into a familiar shape. *I never believed in scrooms,* she heard her own voice speaking but only in her own head. And then there was the soft churring. It was Strix Struma!

*I know, you were never much one for fancies of the imagination, were you, dear?*

For once in her life, Otulissa simply did not know what to say. So she remained quiet. But then a disturbing thought came into her mind and it was almost as if the scroom read it.

*No, I am not unsettled about my life. My business on earth is finished,* the scroom intoned in Otulissa's head. *But there is other business, important business, and it must be settled.*

*What business is that?*

*I'm not sure,* replied Strix Struma.

*Not sure? But you were always sure.*

*Yes, just as you were always sure that there were no such things as scrooms.*

*Please. Can't you tell me? Don't you know at all what it is?*

*And prophecies. You believed that prophecies were somewhat ridiculous.*

The last stanza, Otulissa suddenly thought. And then another thought seemed to pop into her mind, and there was a sensation in her gizzard she had never felt before, like a mighty tug.

*An owl needs me, isn't that so, Strix Struma? The owl I dream of . . .*

The scroom nodded silently.

*Do you know who it is? Please tell me. Who is it?*

But the scroom of Strix Struma began to fade away, and suddenly, the hollow was filled with the bright light of the sun. Otulissa heard the last hiss of her candle as its flame guttered out. But she knew that an owl needed her and that she must go . . . go to Beyond the Beyond. Otulissa knew this not through her usually very rational mind. She knew this because of a dream, a dream she had had several days before of a desperate and very young Barn Owl, almost still a hatchling.

*I have dreamed,* she thought. *I have dreamed!*

The Spotted Owl slept a long, hard, dreamless sleep and did not wake until First Black. And when she did awake, she shook her head. "Simply not so," Otulissa muttered. "It was all just a dream. There is no such thing as scrooms."

But she was aware of the hollow sound of her own words. She walked over to the niches beneath the bookshelves where she kept her charts that showed every region and kingdom in the owl universe with detailed notes on the prevailing winds of each area. She knew what she must do even if she did not know why. "Number thirty-seven, yes, that is the chart I need," she whispered. She drew out a rolled piece of heavy parchment and spread it out on the hollow floor. "Unpredictable thermal volatility," the notes said. "Prevailing winds usually from the southeast except during the eruption seasons. But those seasons are unpredictable as well."

"Yes, yes," Otulissa muttered. "What would one expect from a place like Beyond the Beyond?"

She rolled up the chart carefully after committing the terrain and the pertinent details to memory. She would have to travel light. A few navigation tools, no battle claws, fat lot of good they would do her against dire wolves. *Let's see. What can I give for an excuse?* What would she tell Soren and Gylfie, Digger and Twilight? They would think she had really gone yoicks if she told them that Strix Struma's scroom had shown up after a close reading of the Fire Cycle and she thought she better go directly to Beyond the Beyond. They wouldn't believe her, for one thing. Probably think she was going there to find hireclaws. Ha! This job was way beyond hireclaws! But then she stopped. *What exactly is this job? What am I doing?*

Otulissa for once could not even speculate. She just knew she had to go, and go soon, to Beyond the Beyond. This was in fact beyond rational thought. *Yes*, she thought quietly. *I have dreamed dreams. I have spoken with scrooms. I am desperate. I am dire!*

In a distant forest, another owl crouched low in the hollow of a rotted-out stump and felt the cold shadow of a metal mask pass over him. Nyroc's gizzard clenched in despair. *No, no, it cannot be!*

*Yes!*

He had faced so much. The death of his best friend, the wrath of his mother. He was an owl who could not even fly out into the darkness of the night but must hunt in the glare of the day. *Well, no more!* Nyroc was desperate. He flew out of the stump directly toward the mask that hung in the evening shadows. "You are a mask, you are nothing more! There is nothing behind your mask, not a face, nothing! I shall fly in the fullness of the night. I shall hunt the vole, the rat, even the fox under the moon and the stars. I shall become part of owlkind no matter where I have to go. But go I shall! And I shall never ever return to the Pure Ones. I defy you! I have free will!"

# OWLS
*and others*
*from*

# GUARDIANS *of* GA'HOOLE
*The Hatchling*

### The Band

SOREN: Barn Owl, *Tyto alba,* from the Forest Kingdom of Tyto; escaped from St. Aegolius Academy for Orphaned Owls; a Guardian at the Great Ga'Hoole Tree

GYLFIE: Elf Owl, *Micranthene whitneyi,* from the desert kingdom of Kuneer; escaped from St. Aegolius Academy for Orphaned Owls; Soren's best friend; a Guardian at the Great Ga'Hoole Tree

TWILIGHT: Great Gray Owl, *Strix nebulosa,* free flier, orphaned within hours of hatching; a Guardian at the Great Ga'Hoole Tree

DIGGER: Burrowing Owl, *Speotyto cunicularius,* from the desert kingdom of Kuneer; lost in the desert after attack in which his brother was killed by owls from St. Aegolius; a Guardian at the Great Ga'Hoole Tree

### The Leaders of the Great Ga'Hoole Tree
BORON: Snowy Owl, *Nyctea scandiaca*, the King of Hoole

BARRAN: Snowy Owl, *Nyctea scandiaca*, the Queen of Hoole

EZYLRYB: Whiskered Screech Owl, *Otus trichopsis*, the wise weather-interpretation and colliering ryb (teacher) at the Great Ga'Hoole Tree; Soren's mentor (also known as LYZE OF KIEL)

STRIX STRUMA: Spotted Owl, *Strix occidentalis*, the dignified navigation ryb at the Great Ga'Hoole Tree; killed in the battle against the Pure Ones

SYLVANA: Burrowing Owl, *Speotyto cunicularius*, a young ryb at the Great Ga'Hoole Tree

### Others at the Great Ga'Hoole Tree
OTULISSA: Spotted Owl, *Strix occidentalis*, a student of prestigious lineage at the Great Ga'Hoole Tree, ryb of Ga'Hoolology

MARTIN: Northern Saw-whet Owl, *Aegolius acadicus*, in Ezylryb's chaw with Soren

RUBY: Short-eared Owl, *Asio flammeus*, in Ezylryb's chaw with Soren

EGLANTINE: Barn Owl, *Tyto alba*, Soren's younger sister

MADAME PLONK: Snowy Owl, *Nyctea scandiaca*, the elegant singer of the Great Ga'Hoole Tree

BUBO: Great Horned Owl, *Bubo virginianus*, the blacksmith of the Great Ga'Hoole Tree

MRS. PLITHIVER: Blind snake, formerly the nest-maid for Soren's family; now a member of the harp guild at the Great Ga'Hoole Tree

OCTAVIA: Kielian snake, nest-maid for Madame Plonk and Ezylryb (also known as BRIGID)

The Pure Ones

KLUDD: Barn Owl, *Tyto alba*, Soren's older brother; slain leader of the Pure Ones (also known as METAL BEAK and HIGH TYTO)

NYRA: Barn Owl, *Tyto alba*, Kludd's mate, leader of the Pure Ones after Kludd's death

NYROC: Barn Owl, *Tyto alba*, son born to Nyra and Kludd after Kludd's death, in training to become High Tyto, leader of the Pure Ones

DUSTYTUFT: Greater Sooty Owl, *Tyto tenebricosa*, low-caste owl in the Pure Ones, friend of Nyroc since his hatching (also known as PHILLIP)

WORTMORE: Barn Owl, *Tyto alba*, a Pure One lieutenant

UGLAMORE: Barn Owl, *Tyto alba*, a Pure One sub-lieutenant under Nyra

STRYKER: Barn Owl, *Tyto alba*, a Pure One commander under Nyra

### Other Characters
GWYNDOR: Masked Owl, *Tyto novaehollandiae*, a Rogue smith summoned by the Pure Ones for the Marking ceremony over Kludd's bones

Coming soon!

# GUARDIANS *of* GA'HOOLE

## BOOK EIGHT

### *The Outcast*

by Kathryn Lasky

Haunted by his past and hunted by the Pure Ones, Nyroc flies alone. He yearns to go to the great tree where good and learned owls do noble deeds, but he cannot. He is the son of Kludd and Nyra, sworn enemies of all Ga'Hoole stands for, feared and despised everywhere.

But Nyroc has glimpsed hope — and a new destiny — in the flame over his father's very bones. In search of that destiny, he trains his gaze and turns his beak toward a dark, lawless place where desperate characters roam a barren landscape and fire splits the sky — Beyond the Beyond.

What he does not know is that there is one sent to help him. One who wings away from the great tree against her own reason to help an owl foretold in legend.

# About the Author

KATHRYN LASKY has long had a fascination with owls. Several years ago, she began doing extensive research about these birds and their behaviors — what they eat, how they fly, how they build or find their nests. She thought that she would someday write a nonfiction book about owls illustrated with photographs by her husband, Christopher Knight. She realized, though, that this would be difficult since owls are nocturnal creatures, shy and hard to find. So she decided to write a fantasy about a world of owls. But even though it is an imaginary world in which owls can speak, think, and dream, she wanted to include as much of their natural history as she could.

Kathryn Lasky has written many books, both fiction and nonfiction. She has collaborated with her husband on nonfiction books such as *Sugaring Time*, for which she won a Newbery Honor; *The Most Beautiful Roof in the World*; and most recently, *Interrupted Journey: Saving Endangered Sea Turtles*. Among her fiction books are *The Night Journey*, a winner of the National Jewish Book Award; *Beyond the Burning Time*, an ALA Best Book for Young Adults; *True North; A Journey to the New World; Dreams in the Golden Country*; and

*Porkenstein.* She has written for the My Name Is America series, *The Journal of Augustus Pelletier: The Lewis and Clark Expedition, 1804,* and several books for The Royal Diary series, including *Elizabeth I: Red Rose of the House of Tudor, England, 1544,* and *Jahanara, Princess of Princesses, India, 1627.* She has also received The Boston Globe Horn Book Award as well as The Washington Post Children's Book Guild Award for her contribution to nonfiction.

Lasky and her husband live in Cambridge, Massachusetts.

# Fly beyond the Beyond in a thrilling new adventure...

Guardians of Ga'Hoole #8: *The Outcast* by Kathryn Lasky

**Coming September 2005!**

Young Nyroc has rejected the Pure Ones. And now he flies alone, yearning for something good to believe in. But to prove his goodness, Nyroc must do the unthinkable...give up his name, his inheritance—and even his mother.

Visit the website www.scholastic.com/guardiansofgahoole

# ADVENTURE ABOUNDS IN THESE AWESOME SERIES...

### Gordon Korman

The Falconers are facing life in prison—unless their children, Aiden and Meg, can follow a trail of clues to prove their innocence. Aiden and Meg are on the run, and they must use their wits to make it across the country...with plenty of tests along the way.

### Peter Lerangis

Twins Andrew and Evie navigate a maze of intrigue as they try to uncover the truth about their mother's disappearance in this exciting spy series.

### Emily Rodda

When famine prevails and only monsters thrive, Lief, Barda and Jasmine must rely on their unlikely allies—the last of the Deltora Dragons.

## www.scholastic.com

### ■SCHOLASTIC